Silhouette Books is proud to present

# Annette Broadrick's

$$\boxed{\begin{matrix} 50^{th} \\ book \end{matrix}}$$

## Tall, Dark & Texan

Since 1984, fans worldwide have savored beloved
romance author Annette Broadrick's enormous
talent for writing emotional, entertaining love
stories. Her uplifting novels convey the promise that
in every woman's life there is the possibility
of everlasting love.

### PRAISE FOR ANNETTE BROADRICK

"Annette Broadrick's glorious love stories always
sparkle with irresistible joy and grace."
—Melinda Helfer, *Romantic Times Magazine*

"Annette Broadrick's one terrific writer!"
—Award-winning author Diana Palmer

Dear Reader,

Welcome in the millennium, and the 20th anniversary of Silhouette, with Silhouette Desire—where you're guaranteed powerful, passionate and provocative love stories that feature rugged heroes and spirited heroines who experience the full emotional intensity of falling in love!

We are happy to announce that the ever-fabulous Annette Broadrick will give us the first MAN OF THE MONTH of the 21st century, *Tall, Dark & Texan.* A highly successful Texas tycoon opens his heart and home to a young woman who's holding a secret. Lindsay McKenna makes a dazzling return to Desire with *The Untamed Hunter,* part of her highly successful MORGAN'S MERCENARIES: THE HUNTERS miniseries. Watch sparks fly when a hard-bitten mercenary is reunited with a spirited doctor—the one woman who got away.

*A Texan Comes Courting* features another of THE KEEPERS OF TEXAS from Lass Small's miniseries. A cowboy discovers the woman of his dreams—and a shocking revelation. Alexandra Sellers proves a virginal heroine can bring a Casanova to his knees in *Occupation: Casanova.* Desire's themed series THE BRIDAL BID debuts with Amy J. Fetzer's *Going…Going…Wed!* And in *Conveniently His,* Shirley Rogers presents best friends turned lovers in a marriage-of-convenience story.

Each and every month, Silhouette Desire offers you six exhilarating journeys into the seductive world of romance. So start off the new millennium right, by making a commitment to sensual love and treating yourself to all six!

Enjoy!

Joan Marlow Golan
Senior Editor, Silhouette Desire

Please address questions and book requests to:
Silhouette Reader Service
U.S.: 3010 Walden Ave., P.O. Box 1325, Buffalo, NY 14269
Canadian: P.O. Box 609, Fort Erie, Ont. L2A 5X3

# Annette Broadrick
## Tall, Dark & Texan

Published by Silhouette Books

**America's Publisher of Contemporary Romance**

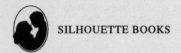 SILHOUETTE BOOKS

ISBN 0-373-76261-5

TALL, DARK & TEXAN

Copyright © 1999 by Annette Broadrick

Visit us at www.romance.net

**Printed in U.S.A.**

## ANNETTE BROADRICK

believes in romance and the magic of life. Since 1984, Annette has shared her view of life and love with readers. In addition to being nominated by *Romantic Times Magazine* as one of the Best New Authors of that year, she has also won the *Romantic Times* Reviewers' Choice Award for Best in its Series, the *Romantic Times Magazine* W.I.S.H. award and *Romantic Times Magazine* Lifetime Achievement Awards for Series Romance and Series Romantic Fantasy.

## To Pam Firle

Who's not only a terrific neighbor, but a great friend.
Thank you for being there for me.

# One

Dan Crenshaw noticed her as soon as she stepped inside the smoke-filled bar. He wasn't the only one. Provocatively dressed in a bright, tropical print strapless dress with her black hair tumbling around her shoulders and down her back, the woman stuck out like an exotic flower in a patch of weeds.

Although small, there was nothing childlike about her. The dress molded her softly rounded body in a seductive manner that would have any red-blooded male baying at the moon.

Her appearance in the small bar screamed trouble waiting to happen, the last thing Dan wanted.

The seedy bar had passed its prime a good forty years ago. Situated in an old building overlooking the bay, its weathered exterior and faded sign didn't lure many first-time visitors to the island to pass through its portals. He had a hunch that whoever she was, she wasn't one of the locals.

Loud music from a local radio station spewed out songs long past their prime, effectively muffling all but the loudest of the conversation at the bar. The place was crowded for a weeknight. Barstools filled with regulars swapping tales of the day crowded around the bar at one end of the room. After everyone looked her over, conversation resumed.

Dan had claimed the back table at the other end of the room for his own since he'd arrived on South Padre Island. He liked coming here because everybody left him alone. Just the way he wanted it.

One morning a few weeks ago, he'd suddenly walked away from his ranch in the Hill Country and his computer business in Austin, as well as his belief in himself, and had headed south. The island was as far south as he could go and stay in Texas and the United States.

Now he sat hunched over his drink, wondering why a woman who looked like that would visit this place. He kept expecting her to discover her mistake and leave. Instead, she leisurely looked around before sauntering toward the group of tables arranged at his end of the room.

The bar area glowed with colored neon lights advertising different brands of beer, leaving the rest of the room in shadows. Hurricane lamps with small candles inside them sat on each of the eight tables, forming small islands of light.

She sat down two tables away from him and placed her purse on the chair beside her. Dan had an excellent view of her profile—a high forehead, patrician nose, pouting mouth, softly rounded chin and long, slender neck.

Laramie, the bartender, tripped all over himself in an effort to get to her and take her order. Dan couldn't hear her voice because of the loud music and conversation, but he expected to see poor ol' Laramie start salivating as he leaned closer to hear her drink preference.

Dan finished his Scotch and lifted his glass to Laramie, signaling the bartender to bring him another one. He studied the ice cubes, wondering if a person could read his fortune in ice as well as tea leaves. It would probably be a lot tougher. He'd have to be quick or all the esoteric signs would melt.

When he glanced up again he discovered the woman's gaze fixed on him. In the smoky, dimly lit room her eyes shone like black jet, the light from the candle reflected in their ebony depths. He lifted his empty glass and sketched a toast in the air.

She eyed him for a moment without changing expression, then looked toward the bar, where Laramie could be seen rushing back to them with a full glass clutched in each hand.

Dan picked up his fresh drink and took a careful sip. He wasn't in the least surprised to be snubbed by the young woman. He probably looked like some pirate who'd recently been found washed up on the beach.

He rubbed his chin thoughtfully, unable to remember the last time he'd shaved, or run a comb through his shaggy, dark hair. None of his employees would recognize him, now. Hell, probably his own sister wouldn't recognize him.

Mandy. Damn. He'd been working hard to put her out of his mind. She'd really ticked him off earlier in the evening, giving him hell over the phone for refusing to return home.

She didn't understand how seductive life on the island could be. He slept when he wanted, ate when he wanted, drank when he wanted. This was the first time in years he'd stayed at the condo. He'd picked it up for a song several years ago when the Mexican market had taken a nosedive, causing the economy along the border between south Texas and Mexico to suffer.

His condo was in the tallest building on the island with a commanding view of both the Gulf of Mexico and the bay that separated the island from Port Isabel.

No, he had absolutely no desire to leave the island. As far as he was concerned, he'd found his new home. He mentally toasted the thought and took a long drink from his new order.

*Well, I found him. Now what?*

Shannon Doyle took a careful sip of her house wine and controlled her reaction. She had a hunch that this particular bar had few requests for wine.

Just a hunch.

Okay. She'd been rehearsing for this meeting for the past three days. Lights! Camera! Action!

Only she couldn't seem to remember her lines.

Shannon fought the urge to tug on the bodice of her dress. When she'd found it that afternoon in one of the island boutiques, she'd whimsically thought it would be just the thing for getting Dan's attention. She hadn't really given enough thought to the amount of attention she was drawing from everyone else in the place.

*All right. Let's face it. I'm not the femme fatale type.* Quite the opposite. Shannon had spent most of her life with her head buried in a book, or glued to a computer screen. She'd never been interested in dressing to attract the attention of the opposite sex.

Good thing, because none of them had ever noticed her, unless they'd needed help with homework when she was in school. Or later—she didn't want to think about later.

She had to chalk up her recent experience with Rick Taylor to her lack of knowledge and understanding of the male animal. Any male animal.

Except for her two brothers, she hadn't been around all that many. Even her cat was female.

When she'd first planned this, she figured that she'd have to do something startling to get Dan to even notice her. Hence, the new dress.

Well, he'd looked at her, all right. His gaze had caused her pulse to accelerate at least twenty points. But he hadn't recognized her.

Not that she would expect him to, of course. That was the point of this exercise, after all. Like a butterfly emerging from its cocoon, Shannon had decided to create a whole new identity for herself.

Maybe she hadn't made a great first choice in men by diving into the dating game with Rick those few months, but after talking to Mandy McClain last week, Shannon had decided that she wouldn't let her disappointment send her running back to her solitary life-style. She intended to follow her heart. Instead of fantasies, she had decided to turn her adolescent dreams into reality.

Dan Crenshaw had been the lover in her dreams since she was thirteen. He'd been a senior in high school then. A football star. Popular and smart and good-looking.

She'd still been struggling with what her mother kindly referred to as baby fat. Baby fat? At thirteen? Well, whatever it was, she'd looked like an aspiring hippo, lumbering along with her friends. The glasses hadn't helped—their thick lenses giving her an owl-like appearance.

Of course she hadn't looked like that in years. By the time she'd gone to college she'd slimmed down and gotten used to contact lenses, but those early years left a definite mark on a person's psyche. There were times when it didn't matter what she saw in the mirror. She felt overweight and ugly.

The dress was supposed to give her self-confidence. Instead, she was afraid its brash exposure might end up giving her hives.

She heard the scrape of a chair and casually glanced around.

Dan was getting up! Oh, no. Not yet. She hadn't made her move yet. Then she noticed that he wasn't headed toward the door. Instead, he ambled over to the bar and spoke to the bartender, who glanced her way and laughed, then proceeded down the hallway toward the rest rooms.

Shannon released the air she'd been hoarding in her lungs with a thankful sigh. She still had time to approach him.

It was a wonder she'd had any air left once she'd gotten a good look at him. She didn't know what he'd looked like before coming here, but the island had certainly burnished him with a sexy bronze finish.

He wore a sleeveless T-shirt with something written on it and a pair of cutoff jeans that lovingly clung to his taut derriere and showed off strong, muscular thighs. He barely met the minimum dress code by wearing flip-flops for shoes.

Not the usual attire for the head of most companies.

She had to agree with Mandy. Something needed to be done.

Shannon was determined not to flunk out on her newest mission—saving Dan Crenshaw from himself.

When Dan returned from the rest room, Laramie had another drink waiting for him at the bar. He snagged the glass between his thumb and middle finger before strolling back to his chair.

The woman was still sipping on her first drink. Wine. That figured.

He sat down and leaned the chair back on two legs, resting against the wall. He was in a particularly foul mood tonight and all because he'd made the mistake of picking up the damned phone when it rang earlier.

"What!" he'd yelled into the receiver after listening to the phone ring off and on most of the afternoon.

"Is that any way to answer a phone?" Mandy asked.

"What do you want?"

"You don't have to be rude."

"And you don't have to spend every waking moment of every stinking day calling to make sure I haven't thrown myself off the balcony."

There was a silence. Finally, Mandy said, "That's not funny, Dan...and it just so happens that I haven't called you in three days."

"No kidding. Hell, you've set a new record. I'll send you a medal."

The silence was longer this time. Much longer. Finally, he heard a sigh. "We need to talk," Mandy said.

"We *are* talking."

"About DSC."

"I told you. I don't want to talk about the company."

"Oh, you've made yourself quite clear about that, big brother. It was so easy for you to shrug your shoulders, walk away and say, 'I quit.' But the world continues on, Dan, even if you decided to step off. You still have contracts to fill, quotas to meet, and there's no one capable of running the place with both you and James gone. You hired Rafe as head of security. He doesn't know a blasted thing about running your stupid company for you."

"Nobody asked him to."

"Well, somebody has to! A national employment

agency has been calling with resumes. They said you'd contacted them and now they want to make appointments for applicants. Nobody knows what to tell them. Rafe isn't qualified to interview people. Forget the fact that the business is losing potential sales because you aren't there, but someone needs to be in the plant making certain that the contracts already signed are being met. If they aren't, you're going to find yourself inundated with lawsuits. For some reason I can't see you enjoying being back in court again.''

"Low blow, Mandy.''

"Everything is a low blow to you these days, Dan, and I, for one, am getting sick and tired of tiptoeing around you. Rafe will never tell you this, but somebody needs to. You've got to stop thinking about your pain and your agony and your loss and start thinking about somebody else for a change. Do you have any idea the hours that Rafe is putting into that company, trying to save your butt? I hardly see him anymore. He rarely gets home before eleven and he's gone by seven every morning. That's no way for anyone to live. I know James hurt you—''

"Hurt me? Hell, Mandy, this isn't about my hurt feelings. He did his damnedest to pin everything he'd done on me! If it hadn't been for Rafe finding the evidence to prove his involvement rather than mine, it would be me sitting in the pen these days and not James.''

"Exactly my point! Yes, James was your friend. And, yes, he betrayed you. Cost you money. Almost bankrupted the company. But he wasn't your only friend. Rafe's been there for you every step of the way. And you don't seem to care that we've all done everything we could think of to make this easier for you. Someone has to deal with the life you decided to toss aside. None of this is just going to fix itself without you.''

"Why didn't Rafe call me and tell me this?"

"When would he have the time?"

Dan couldn't think of a really smart retort to that one. He knew what kind of hours the company demanded. He'd been keeping them for years. And he'd had help back then—from his old college buddy...partner...friend— James Williams. Good ol' James. The lousy, stinking, lying thief.

He didn't want the reminders. He didn't want to be having this conversation. "I'll talk to Rafe," he finally muttered.

"When?"

"Soon."

"How soon?"

"Damn it, Mandy, quit pushing. I said I'd talk to him. Now back off."

"Sometimes you can be such a jerk, Dan."

"I love you, too. Give Angie a hug and a kiss from her Uncle Dan."

"Do it yourself!" she said, slamming down the phone.

He focused on the noisy conversation and music around him, trying to erase the confrontation with Mandy. He couldn't remember her ever being that angry with him before, not even when they were growing up together on the ranch. He lifted his drink to his mouth, trying to wash away the memory.

The problem was that he knew Mandy was right. He was being a jerk. Rafe had come through for him once again. He wondered if his friend—and now his brother-in-law—ever got tired of coming to his rescue.

The scrape of a chair against the cement floor drew his attention and he glanced up from his serious contemplation of his drink. The woman in the sexy sarong stood there at his table, looking down at him. When he finally focused on her face, she gave him a very seductive smile.

"You shouldn't be sitting here all alone, you know," she said in a husky voice. Without waiting for him to respond, she sat across from him and took a slow sip of her drink, her gaze focused on him.

His chair fell back onto all four legs with a resounding thud, jarring him.

He caught a hint of a floral scent that could almost be part of the tropical flowers on her clinging dress. Dan blinked, wondering if he'd fallen asleep without knowing it.

Up close he could see that her skin almost shimmered with the lustrous glow of a fine porcelain figurine. All right, he must really be dreaming. Granted he hadn't been involved with a woman for a while. Maybe the booze had helped his fantasy woman appear to him in living color and fully dimensional.

He placed his hands on the table, cupping his drink protectively, and smiled at her.

She looked startled for a split second before she took another sip from her wine glass, then ran her tongue over her bottom lip in an unconscious gesture that caused his attention to focus on that full, pouty protrusion.

"I've never seen you in here before," he finally said, then almost groaned at the banality of the statement. Yes, he was definitely rusty at this.

She leaned toward him, then lifted her hand and laid it against his cheek. He flinched and jerked back from her touch.

"Did you run out of razor blades?" she murmured.

He nodded toward the bar. "You'll find all the clean shaves you want at the bar, if that's what you prefer."

If possible, her voice dropped to a huskier level. "Why

would I do that, Danny, when you're the one I came so far to find.''

All right, so he'd had too much to drink. That was the only explanation he could come up with to account for a beautiful stranger's apparent interest in him. He had to be imagining this whole thing. But how did this woman know his name?

Peering at her through narrowed eyes, he asked, ''Who the hell are you?''

She sat back in her chair and gave him a smile that would tempt a saint. ''Why Danny, don't you recognize me? I am your worst nightmare.''

# Two

"Oh, I don't think so," he replied, vaguely aware that his body was already responding to her.

She studied him in silence for a couple of moments, then as though speaking to herself, she said, "I think we need to get you home." She stood and took his hand. Giving a slight tug, she smiled and said, "Let's go."

Conversation at the bar lessened. Dan glanced over and saw that most of the gathering was looking his way. Well, why not? He had this gorgeous woman coaxing him to take her home. He still was a little unsure how he'd lucked out, but he wasn't going to question his good fortune.

He slowly stood, a lopsided smile on his face. "Whatever you say, honey," he said.

"My name is Shannon. Think you can remember that?" She wrapped her arm around his waist and steered him to the door. He laughed. Damn. He must be doing something right.

He pushed the door open and stepped outside. A nice breeze caressed the island, coming off the Gulf. Dan took a deep breath, enjoying the fresh air after the closeness of the bar.

A quarter moon hung in midsky, shedding enough light for him to see the surrounding area.

"Great time of the year to be here, isn't it?" he asked, expansively.

She stepped away and watched him as though expecting him to fall over on his face. He took her hand. "I had no idea October would be the perfect time to come to the island. Few tourists, great weather. What more can ya ask?"

"It's November," she replied, leading him toward a small sports car. She opened the passenger door and nodded. "Get in. I'll drive you home."

He nodded wisely and followed her directions. "Good idea. It's a long walk back. Normally I enjoy the walk, but you seem to be in a hurry tonight."

He leaned back in the seat and closed his eyes.

Shannon walked around the car and slid into the driver's seat. She looked over at him and shook her head. *Oh, Dan, what are you doing to yourself?* Now that she was here, she could see why Mandy was so concerned.

Thank goodness she was ready for a little vacation of her own. Dan was right about this time of the year. Seasonal rains hadn't started and it was too early for the winter tourists.

Mandy had told her where the condo was located. She stopped at the gate. "Dan? What's the security code?" She waited. "Dan?"

"Hmph?"

"The security code."

"Oh." He rattled off the numbers. She prayed he'd

remembered the right ones. The gate swung open as soon as she punched them in. So far, so good. She drove to the parking lot, pulled in and parked, then turned to him again.

"Okay, big guy. You've got to help me here."

Dan opened his eyes and sat up, looking around him. "Damn, I keep falling asleep. Or maybe I keep waking up." He looked at her, his smile growing. "Oh yeah. You are definitely a part of my dream."

She tried not to roll her eyes. She got out of the car and came around to his side. He'd managed to get out on his own. He grasped her hand and practically dragged her over to the building's entrance. A security guard recognized him and opened the door.

"Evening, Mr. Crenshaw," the man said.

"Yep," Dan replied without pausing. He marched over to the elevators, punched the button and the door immediately opened. With innate courtesy he waved her inside, then stepped in behind her.

"What floor?" she asked.

"Top one."

"Mmm. Must have a great view."

"Good enough."

Neither spoke until the doors opened and he stepped out ahead of her, fumbling in the pocket of those tight cutoff jeans for the key. Once he opened the door, he made a graceful sweep of his hand. "Welcome to my humble abode."

Humble was a definite misnomer. The place was alight in mirrors, glass and chrome. A sweeping expanse of Berber carpet flowed to walls of glass. She could see a long balcony that wrapped around the outside of the condo.

"Would you like a drink?" he asked.

She turned and saw that he stood behind a wet bar,

holding up a bottle. She smiled, amused despite the circumstances. "Uh, no, thanks. Maybe later."

He flashed that charming smile at her once again, the one that had always made her knees wobble. "Would you like to see the rest of the place?"

She clasped her hands at her waist and nodded. "Please."

He gave her a whirlwind tour of the dining room and kitchen, which was filled with every appliance needed to turn an average cook into a prize chef. She idly peeked into the pantry and the refrigerator.

They were empty.

There were three bedrooms, each with its own complete bath. Well, that would make things a little simpler, she decided, following him into the master bedroom.

Ah, the view from here was spectacular. He could lie in bed and watch the moon as it arced across the sky.

Dan closed the vertical blinds and turned back to her.

"What did you say your name is?"

"Shannon."

"That's a pretty name."

"Thank you."

"How did you know my name?"

"Well, that really wasn't difficult, since I've known you for most of my life." She walked over to the rumpled bed, straightened the covers before turning them back. "Why don't you get some rest? We'll talk in the morning."

He stalked toward her and said, "I don't think either one of us will be getting much rest, do you?" He wrapped his arms around her and found her lips with his.

She hadn't expected him to grab her like that. She struggled, trying to place her hands on his chest. Somewhere along the way the kiss changed, became more seeking, less demanding, and she found herself relaxing in his arms.

This was Dan, after all. He would never take advantage of her. Besides, wasn't this exactly the fantasy she'd lived with for years? However, he didn't need to know that, and she sure wasn't going to let him think that he'd successfully seduced her.

With a quick twist away from him she stepped back, trying to catch her breath and maintain her composure, as well. There was no reason for him to know that she didn't have much experience in the seduction department.

Her sudden evasion caused him to lose his balance. Luckily he fell forward and ended up facedown on the bed.

He didn't move.

She ventured closer. He was sprawled across the bed, his head on the far pillow, his body angled so one foot dangled over the side. He'd lost his flip-flops. She studied him for a moment, then decided to leave him there. She draped a light blanket across him and left the room, quietly closing the door behind her.

Shannon spotted the phone in the living room. This was as good a time as any to contact Mandy. She took the cordless phone out onto the balcony and sank into one of the comfortably padded chairs. She punched in the numbers from memory, then listened to the phone ring at the other end of the line.

As soon as Mandy answered, Shannon said, "Hi, this is Shannon. Mission accomplished. I found Dan this evening."

The relieved sigh from the other end winged its way to her ear. "Thank God. How is he?"

Shannon smiled to herself. "He could best be summed up as having gone native. He might not have gone as far as the South Seas, but he looks like your typical beach-comber.''

''Has he lost weight?''

''Now that, I couldn't tell you. Remember, I haven't seen him in several years. I must say, he looks healthy enough to me.''

''I've been so worried. I managed to get in touch with him earlier today and we had a horrible fight.''

''Well, he didn't give me any trouble. I found him at a local hangout and suggested we come back to his place.''

''Oh, good. Did he recognize you?''

''Are you kidding? He hasn't a clue who I am or why I'm here. I have a hunch he won't be nearly so happy to see me come morning.''

Mandy sighed once more. ''I really don't know what to do anymore, Shannon. And Rafe's no help. He says everyone at the plant is very understanding of the situation. Thank goodness there are good shift managers who can oversee what needs to be done without supervision.''

''I can understand your concern. After all, I have a couple of big brothers, too. If either of them went off the deep end like this, I'd be worried sick as well.''

''I can't begin to tell you how much I appreciate your volunteering to look after him for me.''

Shannon laughed. ''I have a hunch the job's going to get much tougher when morning rolls around. But I can handle him. As I said, I'm used to dealing with my brothers.''

''I hope you'll be able to enjoy the island, as well.''

''Oh, I certainly intend to do that. I haven't been down here in more than five years. I have some serious sunbathing to do.''

"I'm sure once Dan gets his act together, he'll thank you for what you're doing for him."

"I won't hold my breath. Besides, I'm still hoping to fill one of the positions currently being offered at his company. So if he's feeling all that appreciative, he can hire me."

"Ah," Mandy replied with a chuckle. "Your ulterior motive reveals itself."

"Absolutely. Of course he may never want to lay eyes on me again after this little jaunt, but that doesn't matter. I was unemployed when I offered to do this. He can't fire me since he hasn't hired me."

"He'll be furious when he finds out I sent you down there."

"Oh, he won't hear it from me. I'll keep in touch. Take care. I'll talk to you soon."

Shannon hung up, found the key to the apartment and went back downstairs to her car, where she got her luggage out of the trunk. The security man helped her with it, made certain she managed to get the pieces inside the elevator and waved her off.

All the way up the elevator she couldn't help but wonder what the guy must be thinking, since Dan hadn't come back down to help her. Maybe she'd introduce herself as his sister. Not that it mattered what he thought. Unless, of course, Dan wanted to protect his own reputation.

Back in the condo, she chose one of the guest bedrooms and unpacked before showering and getting ready for bed. First thing tomorrow she'd go to the grocery store. Well, maybe not first thing. Her favorite occupation whenever she was on the island was to get up at daylight and walk to the jetties to watch the sunrise.

She had a hunch Dan wouldn't be stirring that early.

After that, however, she would be off and running, doing what she could to make Dan's life on the island a living hell.

What, after all, were real friends for?

# Three

Ah, yes, this was the part of life on the island she had missed, Shannon thought the next morning as she strolled along the beach. A few early risers were also out—some jogging, others looking for shells. She took in a slow, deep breath of air, reveling in the fresh scent of the sea.

Shannon had spent the past three years working in St. Louis, spending her winter vacations on the Colorado ski slopes. She'd missed the sensuous pleasure of walking barefoot over a damp, hard-packed, sandy beach.

While on her shopping spree yesterday she'd indulged herself by purchasing a two-piece swimsuit with matching cover-up. Before leaving the apartment this morning, she'd taken the time to braid her hair into a single plait. The mirror had revealed that she was much too pale. She had every intention of soaking up some sun later today after she ran her errands.

In the meantime, she was content to pick up unusual

shells and slip them in her pockets. By the time she reached the jetties, she had a nice collection.

She climbed up on the granite boulders so that she could see the channel that led to the seaport farther inland. There were large birds—she recognized pelicans and egrets, but others she wasn't so sure about—fishing along the edges.

There were also human fishermen with their rods and reels casting off of either side of the granite ledge. Shannon walked out a short distance and found a spot where she could sit and watch as the sun burst fully into view.

She gave herself up to the moment.

Eventually, the time came when she knew she had to get started with her day. With a great deal of reluctance, and a mental promise to return in time for sunset, Shannon focused on her reason for being on the island—Dan Crenshaw.

She listened for him when she let herself into the apartment, but heard nothing. The door to his room was closed. She peeked inside the darkened interior and saw him still asleep.

So. First things first. She quickly made up a grocery list and left for the store. After buying basic essentials and enough food for a few simple meals, she returned. Still no sign of his stirring.

Shannon made coffee, began frying bacon, and mixed up an herbal concoction for Dan. She had a hunch he might have a bit of a headache this morning.

The sun was now up in all its glory, flooding the large living room with light. She tapped softly on his door but when he didn't answer she opened the door and stepped inside.

Dan now lay on his back, his arms thrown wide. He

looked very good to her from what she could see in the dim light.

She sat the steaming cup beside the bed and walked over to the blinds. She got an immediate response as soon as she pulled the shades open.

"Wha—? Shut the damn blinds! What do you think you're doing?"

She turned and found him sitting up in the middle of the bed, his elbows resting on his drawn-up knees, his face buried in his hands.

"Good morning!" she said, brightly. "I brought you something to drink."

His head jerked up at the sound of her voice.

"Who—what are you doing here?"

Crossing her fingers behind her back, she grinned and said, "Why, you invited me to stay here with you...don't you remember?"

He groaned an answer.

She picked up the cup. "Here. This should help."

He reached for it with a trembling hand. He sniffed, then made a face. Squinting into the cup, he asked, "What is it?"

"Oh, my very special formula for late nights and over-indulging."

"I never overindulge," he stated with dignity.

"That's good to hear," she replied, turning away. "Breakfast is almost ready."

"Good grief, this stuff tastes vile! What are you trying to do, poison me?"

She stopped at the doorway and looked over her shoulder. "Now there's a thought. If you're going to be a baby, then don't drink it." She closed the door softly behind her.

Dan felt as though he'd awakened in some kind of

nightmare. He didn't remember leaving the bar last night. He didn't remember coming back to the condo. And he certainly didn't remember anyone like the woman who'd just walked out of his bedroom.

She wore a pair of bright yellow shorts that revealed shapely legs, a yellow halter top that displayed more than a little cleavage and long earrings of brightly painted macaws. Her black hair was pulled back from her face in an intricate braid, and her black eyes seemed filled with amazing good humor.

What the hell was going on?

He forced himself to drink the steaming, and very bitter, herbal tea. Not that he wanted it or even needed it. Granted he had the granddaddy of all headaches this morning, but he was certain that was due to too much sun yesterday.

He felt his way into his bathroom and stared into the mirror. Why had he slept in his clothes last night?

Well, at least that reassured him about one thing—he hadn't made love to the seductive stranger who seemed to have made herself at home in his place. Why couldn't he remember her?

With that thought he had a sudden image of sitting in the bar and watching an exotic-looking woman come in wearing a red, saronglike dress. That's all he remembered—a brief burst of memory, like a camera flash.

Maybe he'd had a little more to drink last night than he'd thought. He didn't remember settling up his tab with Laramie, but he knew that wasn't a problem. He could go back to the bar today, or pay it this evening when he was there. The place had become a hangout for him lately.

Dan stripped out of his clothes and stepped into the shower. He needed something to get him going. Somehow he was going to have to explain to the unknown woman that whatever he may have said to her last night, she couldn't stay with him.

He'd never had much time for relationships, especially in the past few years. A broken engagement had taught him a valuable lesson—most women wanted more of his time and attention than he had available. He closed his eyes and let the spray hit him in the face.

He hadn't thought of Sharon in a long while. He'd been really shaken when she'd called off the wedding just a few weeks before the ceremony was to take place. The problem, he'd realized many months later, was that he had been unprepared for her sudden decision. She'd never hinted there was a problem. In fact, the reason he'd been putting in the long hours was because of the three-week honeymoon they'd planned to take.

That's when he realized how little he understood women. He could deal with them quite well in a business setting, but socially he hadn't a clue what to say to them.

What had happened to him last night that had caused him to brave rejection by inviting his visitor home with him? And why had she said yes?

By the time he was out of the shower, he'd firmly re-solved to get some of his questions answered. But first, maybe he ought to shave. He rubbed his jaw thoughtfully. He could pass as Blackbeard the pirate at the moment. Not exactly what he'd had in mind for a dress code—even for his new vacation-style way of life.

Shaving took longer than usual. Damn, he wondered how long it had been since he'd bothered?

He also noticed his stomach growl a couple of times. He hadn't been hungry in a long time. Maybe it had some-thing to do with that horrible herbal drink.

He returned to the bedroom and slipped into a pair of briefs and a faded pair of jeans. He grabbed a pullover shirt out of the drawer, one of the last clean ones, and reminded himself to wash some clothes today.

When he opened the bedroom door he smelled the scent of bacon and coffee. A heavenly combination if he'd ever smelled one. He followed his nose into the kitchen area and discovered the small table there had been set for two.

"My, don't you look nice," the woman said when he walked through the door.

Dan rubbed his chin self-consciously. "Thanks," he muttered. He looked at the table. "Uh, this is really nice of you, but you didn't have to go to all this trouble."

"It's no trouble." She poured a glass of orange juice and handed it to him. "How do you like your coffee?"

"Mmm, black." Dan couldn't figure this out. He could swear he didn't know this woman and yet she was acting as though they'd lived together for years.

He sat down and she placed a steaming plate of food in front of him. His stomach did a little flip and he closed his eyes. "I'm not sure—" he began, but she cut him off.

"Eat. It's the best thing for what ails you. You'll be amazed how much better you'll feel once you get something solid inside you."

He rubbed his forehead, where little sledgehammers still tapped rhythmically. He wasn't up to the argument. He picked up the coffee as soon as she set it down and sipped.

Ah, that definitely helped.

When the woman sat across from him he forced himself to meet her eyes. He got caught up in their size and shape and color. Large and black and slightly tilted, which gave her a very exotic look. He gave his head a quick shake. What difference did it make what her eyes looked like?

"I'm a little hazy about last night," he finally muttered. She gave him a brilliant smile. "Oh, you have absolutely nothing to apologize for, Dan. You were wonderful! I'll never forget it.''

He leaned back in his chair and looked at her with irritation. ''Wonderful, huh?''

She nodded with enthusiasm and began to eat.

''Exactly what did I do that was so wonderful?''

That seemed to give her pause. She finished chewing, took a dainty sip of juice—which triggered another memory—of her sipping from a wineglass—before looking at him with eyes that sparkled in the morning light. ''Well,'' she said slowly, ''I don't know how I could single out one particular thing.'' She gave a little wave of her hand.

''Try,'' he replied, deciding to nibble on a little of the toast and bacon. He took a bite and was relieved to find it not only tasted good, but also had a very good chance of staying down. He was encouraged.

''Well, you just—sort of—swept me off my feet. I couldn't resist you. I—'' She paused and watched him munch on a piece of toast. ''You don't believe me, do you?''

''Not a word,'' he assured her, taking a bite of egg with bacon.

''Oh.''

''So what is this all about? Who are you and why are you here?''

She studied him for a long moment, then sighed. ''You really don't remember, do you?''

He finished off the egg and another piece of toast before he said, ''I remember enough to know that I was neither irresistible nor able to sweep you off your feet. I was doing well to navigate with my own two feet.''

She laughed.

It caught him off guard. She had a delightful, husky chuckle that felt like little fingers running up and down his spine. He straightened and reached for another piece of toast.

She jumped up and returned with the coffeepot, refilling both their cups.

When she sat down again she leaned her chin on her hands and asked, "Do you remember Buddy Doyle?"

He stared at her, for the first time wondering if she was a mental case. If so, he would have to handle her very carefully.

"Buddy Doyle?" he repeated.

"Uh-huh."

"The only Buddy Doyle I know was a guy I knew back in high school. He was one of the best—and the biggest— defensive linemen on our football team for three years running."

She smiled, as though delighted with him. "That's Buddy. I'm his kid sister, Shannon."

"Buddy Doyle is your brother."

"Yes."

"And what does Buddy Doyle have to do with your being here with me?"

"Absolutely nothing."

"I see." He wished to hell he did. This was becoming more bizarre with every moment.

"I was behind you a few years in school," she prompted.

"You're from Wimberley?"

"That's where I attended school. We had a ranch south of there."

Dan's ranch was north of Wimberley. He didn't remember Shannon at all. He would definitely have remembered her if they'd gone to school together. She was not the type of woman a man could easily forget.

"So what are you doing here?"

"Well, I've recently moved back to Texas, and I was looking for a job. I answered an ad in the Austin paper and discovered that you were the owner of the company, but that you were away on vacation. I thought that since I hadn't had a vacation in a few years, myself, I would come down to the island for a few days. You can imagine my surprise when I saw you at that bar last night. It was like fate had thrown us together."

He carefully placed his utensils on his now empty plate and folded his arms. "Let me get this straight. You're here to interview for a job?"

Her infectious laugh cascaded in musical peals around him. "Oh, no. I'm going to enjoy the island for a while. I'll wait until you get back to Austin to set up an interview."

"I have no idea when that will be."

"I'll wait."

He eyed her with misgiving. "I don't want to be rude, Ms. Doyle, but I don't want you staying here."

Her smile was sunny. "My name is Shannon and I promise not to get in your way. I'll be happy to prepare your meals, and do a little housework for you. You have a lovely place here. It will be a pleasure."

"Look, if you need money for a hotel room, I can probably help you out there."

"That's so kind of you to offer, but this will do just fine. You go on about your routine. Just pretend I'm not here, okay?"

With that she bounced out of her chair and efficiently gathered up their dishes. Dan could feel his jaw drop in astonishment.

Granted, he didn't know much about women, but surely this one was being more than a little brazen.

"Do you expect me to sleep with you?" he asked coldly.

She spun around and stared at him for a moment before offering him a jaunty smile. "Oh, no. That wasn't part of the agreement."

"Then maybe you'd better explain the agreement."

"I'm going to be your housekeeper until you're ready to go back to Austin."

"Do you mind if I take a look around?" he asked politely.

"Seems to me you've been doing just that ever since you came down here." She picked her way back to the original path.

Dan watched until she disappeared around the bend of the road, then he turned and started toward the bank.

# Four

"**Y**ou must be out of your mind," he muttered. "I don't need a housekeeper."

She patted his hand. "Well, let's see how it goes for the next few days, all right?"

"No! It isn't all right. I came down here to be alone. Being alone would preclude having a housekeeper."

"Don't worry. You won't even know I'm around."

"Oh, right," he replied, heavy on the sarcasm.

"What do you usually do at this time of day, Dan?"

Did she have to sound so blasted reasonable? He was feeling anything but reasonable at the moment. He made himself pause and get a grip on his rapidly escalating temper before he spoke.

Finally, he said, "I'm usually asleep at this time of day," he said through a clenched jaw.

She smiled. "Well, now that you know what you've been missing, you should be thankful I got you up. How about a walk on the beach at dawn tomorrow? That's my favorite time of day on the island. You'll love it.''

"My God, haven't you heard anything I've said? I don't want you here!"

She finished loading the dishwasher before she turned around and faced him. "Don't worry. I'll grow on you. Eventually." Then she had the absolute nerve to walk out of the room humming.

He sat there, seething.

All right, enough already. He'd call security and have them get her out of here.

Oh, that would look good. Order security to remove a woman who was scarcely tall enough to come to his shoulder. As though she were some kind of threat to him.

Actually, she *was* a threat to his peace of mind. He didn't need the aggravation. He stomped into the living room and went out onto the balcony. Actually, the day looked quite pleasant. Not many people on the beach.

Maybe he'd go down for a swim. He hadn't bothered to get out much since he'd arrived. Hell, the first week he'd been here all he'd done was sleep, almost around the clock.

The trial had taken its toll on him, that was certain. Helping to convict his long-time friend and business partner for stealing from their own company had been an exhausting nightmare. But it was over now and he had the rest of his life ahead of him. It was no one's fault that his life no longer seemed to have any direction.

Nor did he particularly care.

He went back inside and marched down the hall to his bedroom. Shannon met him in the doorway with her arms full of linens and towels. She gave him a nod and a smile and eased past him.

All right, so maybe he did need to get some chores

done. Laundry hadn't been a priority for him. He changed into swim trunks, found a lone towel in the cabinet and took it. Without comment he left the condo, went downstairs and outside.

Chairs conveniently tucked beneath umbrellas clustered the beach in front of the high-rise building. He found an empty one, tossed the towel on it, then stalked to the water and waded in. He forced himself to keep going, despite the shock of the temperature to his warm body. At the moment, it was just what he needed—to cool off and to figure out what the hell he was going to do about his unwanted guest.

Meanwhile, Shannon was upstairs on the phone with Mandy.

"You made him angry?" his sister repeated worriedly.

"I worked hard at it and I believe my efforts were successful."

"I suppose that's better than the apathy he's been going through."

"It would help if I understood what was going on with him," Shannon said. "You told me that he'd had some business setbacks, and yet the company seems to be growing."

"Oh, I forgot you haven't been here for the past few years. There was this huge investigation going on about the company. It started a couple of years ago. It seems that Dan's partner, James Williams, was secretly taking microprocessor chips from the company, reporting them stolen, then helping to smuggle them out of the country so they could be sold to some Middle Eastern countries with whom the U.S. is no longer doing business of any kind."

"Oh, my."

"Yes. And when he finally got caught—thanks to

Rafe's sleuthing, by the way—James had set it up to look as if Dan was the one responsible for the thefts. He'd even arranged for the stuff to be picked up here on the ranch. Things really looked bad for Dan for a while. Since Rafe knew there was no way Dan could be involved, he just kept digging until he found out the truth. But it was really hard on Dan. He'd been friends with James for years. And of course he trusted him implicitly. So this has been really tough on him.''

''Well, that does explain a few things. He's probably suffering from a form of burnout.''

''That's what Rafe says. He says we should just leave him alone until he's ready to face the daily grind again.''

''Does Rafe know I'm down here?''

''Oh, no. I mean, he knows you came in for an interview. In fact, I think you met him when you were in the office, didn't you?''

''Yes. I remembered him from school. I had no idea the two of you had gotten married, though, until he happened to mention being related to Dan through marriage.''

Mandy laughed. ''I think he's still in shock, as well. I was so glad you called me, though. It was good to hear from you after all this time.''

''I'm glad I did, too. We had a lot to get caught up on.''

''Rafe's going to kill me for encouraging you to go down there, but I don't care. I feel so much better knowing that someone is with him. I guess it's encouraging to know Dan cares enough to get angry. First at me yesterday and now you today.''

Shannon chuckled. ''Well, I have a hunch that I'll be able to keep him on edge for a while longer, at least until he orders me out of here in no uncertain terms.''

"Hang tough, Shannon. And thanks again for caring enough to check on him."

"Oh, that's never been my problem where Dan's concerned. I guess I've had him on some kind of pedestal all these years. It's good to be able to see him as a person with faults and frailties of his own."

Mandy laughed. "Yeah. The trouble with putting someone on a pedestal is you have a much better view of his butt. And he can certainly be one at times."

"Well, I've almost got the place straightened up now. He's really not a messy person, at all. Once I finish this last load of clothes I intend to go soak up some sun. And harass your brother a little more."

"Thanks for checking in this morning. I had my first good night's sleep since he left. Believe me, you've been a real gift."

"Dan definitely doesn't see it that way. But we'll worry about that later. 'Bye now."

Shannon finished folding laundry, then changed back into her bathing suit. After slathering her skin with a heavy sunscreen, she grabbed a towel, a novel she'd brought with her and her sunglasses and went downstairs.

More people were on the beach now than when she'd been there earlier. She spotted an empty chair and settled into it. Not wanting to burn on her first outing, she opened the beach umbrella knowing that she would still be exposed to enough sun to get tan from the reflection off the water.

She read for a while, then closed the book and settled in for a short nap before the time came to start lunch. If nothing else, Dan had lucked out in the culinary department because she loved to cook. Unfortunately, she also loved to eat, which meant a constant battle to exercise off the pounds. The bane of being small-boned and short in stature was that every extra pound showed.

Shannon allowed the soft sound of the rhythmic waves washing up on shore to soothe her into a deep sleep.

Dan had forgotten how enjoyable it was to swim in the Gulf. Careful of the undertow, he found deeper troughs between the sandbars close to shore to really push himself. He hadn't realized how out of shape he'd gotten these past weeks. It felt good to work his body.

Eventually he walked along the shore in knee-deep water and watched the surf fishermen pull in small sharks. He lost track of time until his stomach rumbled. He was actually hungry again.

It would be too much to hope for to find that his new unappointed, uninvited and unwelcome housekeeper had left. He was pleasantly tired after his workout this morning. A good meal and a nap would suit him just fine. She'd obviously been to the grocery store. So maybe she'd already prepared something for lunch. If not, he could always dig around in the refrigerator for sandwich material.

He was approaching the high-rise when he noticed three men talking to a woman seated in one of the chairs near where he'd left his towel. As he drew closer he discovered the woman was Shannon and whatever one of the men was saying had caused her to violently disagree. He couldn't hear what was being said, but she was vehemently shaking her head no, which appeared clear enough to Dan.

Hah. Now maybe she'd find out what it was like to deal with someone who wouldn't take no for an answer.

He took another look at the men. They didn't look much like the usual beach-loving types. They wore bright, vacation-type shirts and shorts, but they were too pasty-colored to have spent much time in the sun. The true give-away was the footwear—all three men wore black socks and lace-up shoes.

Dan wondered if he should interfere. Maybe this was some guy she'd been dating who didn't want to give her up. Dan supposed that would be possible. If he weren't in the middle of some kind of nervous breakdown, he'd probably have welcomed her into his wayward life.

In fact, he realized that despite the fact he'd just met her, Dan felt a little possessive where she was concerned. He didn't like the idea that someone was pursuing her, particularly since it was obvious she wasn't encouraging his attentions.

The man doing all the talking suddenly grabbed Shannon by her upper arm and jerked her to her feet, which forced Dan into taking action. Whatever the guy's beef, there was no reason to manhandle her.

He picked up his pace and trotted toward them.

"Hold it," he hollered as he drew close. "That's no way to treat a lady!"

The other two men spun around and shifted so that they stood between him and the other two. "Stay out of this," one of them said in a guttural voice. "It's none of your business."

Dan had never liked bullies. He didn't really assess the situation before moving closer. He was more concerned with how she was handling all of this.

"Shannon?" he asked. "Are you okay?"

Her answer, sounding shaky, alarmed him. "Uh, not really. I don't have any idea who these men are or what they want, I just—"

"Don't give me that," the man holding her arm said. "We told you we're looking for Rick Taylor. We happen to know the two of you are pretty thick, so don't try to deny it. You've led us on a long chase, lady, so don't play games with me, 'cause I'm not in the mood.''

Dan attempted to step closer, but one of the men blocked his way. He shoved him aside and grabbed the man holding Shannon, forcing him to let her go. "Leave her alone," he said, doubling his fists. He was more than ready to lay him out.

Dan couldn't remember the last time his anger had overcome him. Only now, there was an object to his anger, somebody with whom he could face-off.

Shannon screamed a warning of sorts at the same time Dan felt a blinding pain in the back of the head. He stumbled and fell to his hands and knees, which increased his ire. What the hell was going on? Who did these goons think they were, assaulting people?

He attempted to stand when he was hit on the head again. This time, he went down for the count.

# Five

The first thing Dan became aware of when he regained consciousness was a nauseating, rocking movement and the fact that his head felt as though it was on the verge of exploding.

The second thing he noticed was the sound of an engine droning somewhere nearby, and a soft, scented pillow for his head. From those pieces of information he managed to figure out that he was on a boat, going somewhere.

He tried to move his head and intense pain shot through him.

He groaned.

"Oh Dan, I'm so sorry to get you involved in this mess. Are you okay?"

Shannon. He would recognize that voice anywhere and at the moment it was only a few inches above him. He forced one eye open and saw her very worried face staring back at him.

She was crouched on the floor of the boat where he lay sprawled, holding his head against her breast.

*What the hell had happened?* Since she didn't respond he decided he must have just thought the question. He licked his dry lips and forced his other eye to open. ''Wha's—'' Was that his voice? He sounded drunk. He tried again. ''Wha' happened?''

''One of those men hit you on the head. Twice! They carried you between them to a car where another man was waiting. He looked surprised to see us and started asking them what was going on. He said something about just hiring out his boat and car to them and that he wasn't going to be a part of any assault and kidnapping.

''While the man who seemed to be their leader talked to him in a low voice, the other two loaded you in the back of the car. By then I was determined to stay with you. I mean, they had no reason to hit you! They said they'd been looking for me. I don't know what's going on, but I didn't want you disappearing on me.''

''How long have I been out?''

She thought about it for a moment and said, ''It seems like forever, but I suppose it's been about thirty minutes or so. Long enough for them to bring us to this boat, stow us down here and leave the marina. From the sounds I would guess we're heading out into the Gulf.''

''You've got to be kidding,'' he murmured. Anything louder and his head protested. ''We've been kidnapped?''

She smoothed his hair away from his forehead, her eyes filled with shadows. ''I'm afraid so.''

He closed his eyes. The irony of the situation was almost more than he could take. How many times in a lifetime could a man expect to be kidnapped and live to tell about it? He'd been kidnapped when he first found out his ranch was being used to smuggle microprocessor chips out of the country. He wondered if he had a sign tattooed on his forehead signaling his availability to would-be captors.

"Who are they?" he asked after several minutes of silence.

"I have no idea. I've never seen them before. They may be from St. Louis, since they were asking me about Rick."

"Who's Rick?"

She sighed. "Rick Taylor. I went out with him a few times, then broke up with him. He became a real pest after that, and I finally decided that it wasn't worth staying there and trying to deal with him when I was also getting fed up with some of the problems at work." She stroked his cheek and jaw. "So I decided to return to Texas and look for work in the Austin area. I can't believe that I'm still having problems because of Rick Taylor!"

Dan reached up and gingerly touched the back of his head. His fingers came away covered with blood. "*You're* having problems?" he repeated.

He had to admit that lying against her like this made his pain lessen, somewhat, and he knew that he would forever think of her whenever he smelled that particular floral scent.

"So tell me about this guy Rick," he said, hoping to concentrate on something other than the throbbing pain in his head.

"Well, he was very good-looking, charming, seemed to have lots of money. He always maintained that he worked in investments, but that was a little too vague for me. After I was with him a few times, I began to be really uncomfortable. He made me nervous. I didn't like some of the people he hung around with."

"I can certainly understand that, if these are a few of his friends."

"I've never seen these men before."

"They seem to think you know where Rick is, which sounds as if he might be missing."

"I haven't spoken to Rick in almost three months, so I have no idea where he might be. As far as I know, he's still in St. Louis."

"Something tells me he isn't or they wouldn't have come looking for you." Dan attempted to sit up and a sharper pain shot through his head like a bullet. And to think that he'd been complaining of having a headache when he woke up this morning. He'd had no idea what pain could be like.

Well, this was just great. Here they were being carried out to sea for who knew what purpose, wearing nothing but their swimsuits. He noticed that she wore her cover-up jacket over her suit, but since it was sheer enough to see through, it wasn't going to give her much protection.

He had less than that. He shivered. He hoped to hell he wasn't going into shock.

Shannon said, "I found a towel down here and used it to tend to your wound. It really scared me to see so much blood. It seems to be doing better now."

"I suppose I should thank you for looking after me," he replied, knowing he sounded grumpy but feeling unable to hide his pain and irritation at their situation.

"Or you could blame me for the predicament we're in. Either way, I suppose we've got to make the best of it."

He forced himself to sit up. The movement made his head continue to swim and his stomach roll. He hoped to hell he didn't throw up and utterly humiliate himself.

"Why don't you just lie still? Your color isn't too good at the moment," Shannon offered.

"Can't imagine why." Once upright, he propped his head in one hand while he held the towel to the back of his head with the other, and contented himself by shifting his eyes to see what he could see. They were in some kind of cabin cruiser that had seen a lot of use. He could feel the steady thump of the waves hitting the bottom of the boat, and the throttle sounded as though it was running fully open.

He didn't know how much time they had before their captors reappeared. Someway, somehow he had to be ready to defend them. He needed time to pull himself together.

Shannon watched him with a worried expression on her face. Well, that was reassuring. She was worried about him. That made everything all right, then.

He'd known from the minute he'd laid eyes on her that this woman was trouble. The sudden flashback from the night before was a vivid memory, even if other parts of the evening remained hazy.

Nothing that had happened to him since then caused him to change his mind.

He fought to concentrate on their situation. "Did anyone happen to mention where we're being taken?"

"I heard something about Guardino's yacht, at least that's what it sounded like." She stood and looked down at him. "Are you sure you should be stirring? That was quite a blow you took."

He pushed himself up enough to slide onto one of the bench seats at a small table. Shannon quickly sat down across from him.

"I think I'll live, but I'll probably be a little more reticent in the future about leaping to the rescue the next time I see some guy hassling a woman."

She appeared amused by his disgruntled tone. "Well,

you did take on three of them,'' she reminded him with more than a hint of admiration in her voice.

Not that he cared to gain her admiration, but it helped to salve his ego a little to realize that he *had* gone up against large odds. The truth was that it never occurred to him that the men would actually attack him without a fair fight.

Then again, it hadn't occurred to him that he would be shot and kidnapped when he confronted the smugglers using his ranch as an airstrip, either.

He supposed the lesson he needed to learn was not to be quite so impulsive.

It was his own fault for barreling in and giving orders.

He and Shannon were in a very vulnerable position. He wondered why no one had tried to stop the men from taking them. Of course, at this time of year, there weren't many people on the beach. No one knew where they were. It would be easy enough to toss them overboard without anyone ever finding out what happened to them.

Up until now, he'd been thoroughly convinced that he no longer cared whether he lived or died.

Only now did he discover that he had a definite opinion on the matter—just when the decision seemed to have been taken out of his hands.

He felt badly about his last conversation with Mandy. He hoped he'd have the chance to see her again to apologize. Looking at it from his new perspective, he could see where she'd had to put up with a lot from him these past several months. In fact, both Rafe and Mandy had been extremely patient with him.

What he'd needed was a good swift kick in the pants.

He supposed a couple of knots on the back of his head worked just as well. This little jaunt had certainly gotten his attention.

Shannon got up and peered through the porthole across from them, displaying her curvaceous derriere and slender legs to his view. He closed his eyes. This was no time to be reminded of his attraction to her. Wasn't that what had gotten him into this mess in the first place?

Not that he could remember all of the details, but he figured he must have invited her back to his place with him and somehow given her the impression she could stay on as his housekeeper.

What red-blooded male wouldn't have?

He pulled the towel away from his head and carefully touched his wound again. He seemed to have stopped bleeding. He turned and tried the faucet in the sink behind him, relieved when a trickle of water came out. He held the towel beneath the water.

Shannon turned and looked at him. "What are you doing?"

"I thought I'd try to wash some of the blood off the back of my head."

She returned to his side. "Here. Let me help." She took the towel and carefully dabbed the back of his head, her breasts brushing against his shoulder. He shivered and pulled away. "I'm sorry," she said. "I didn't mean to hurt you."

"Uh, you didn't. No worse than usual. I'm just a little chilled, that's all."

"Maybe I can find something for you to put on," she said. She lifted the bench seat where she'd been sitting and dug around inside. With a soft cry of triumph she pulled out a navy wool sweater. She held it up to her nose and sniffed, then made a face. "It's a little musty but seems clean enough." She shook it out and handed it to him. "I think it should fit. At least it should help you from getting too chilled."

Grateful that she'd found something, he slid it over his head, wincing when it came into contact with his wound. He was lowering it over his face when he heard her say something that was muffled by the sweater.

"What did you say?" he asked, settling it around his waist. He hadn't realized how cold he'd become and was grateful for the warmth.

"I've been meaning to ask you ever since I first saw you in your bathing suit this afternoon. How did you get the scar on your shoulder?"

He smiled ruefully. "As a matter of fact, that's a little memento I picked up a few years ago when I decided to challenge some smugglers who were using my ranch for their pickup-and-delivery depot."

Her eyes widened. "They shot you?"

"To be honest, I don't think it was intentional. I startled them. They were deliverymen whose boss thought I'd agreed to the arrangement, so they weren't expecting to be confronted."

"How badly were you hurt?"

"Bad enough. They could have left me there, I suppose, and maybe my ranch foreman would have come looking for me the next day, but as it turned out, they loaded me in their plane and flew me back to Mexico with them." He shook his head, thinking about his other kidnapping adventure. He certainly hoped this one didn't get as complicated as the last one had.

"You're lucky it didn't kill you."

"Yes, I am. Very lucky. The problem was that the wound became infected and there weren't any antibiotics around to treat it. I was in pretty bad shape when Rafe found me a few weeks later."

"Rafe McClain," she said. "You two were really close in high school, I remember that."

"Yes. He literally saved my life."

"Too bad he can't help us now," she said, peering out the porthole again. "Oh! I think I see something. A ship. A yacht, really. Very nice."

He felt the cruiser begin to lessen its speed and heard someone hail the ship. He reminded himself not to make any hasty moves. Playing hero could get a guy killed, which was damned permanent.

"Well, looks like we've arrived at our destination," Dan said, determined not to scare Shannon with his opinion of their chances.

She turned and faced him. "I know this is cowardly to admit, but I'm glad I'm not here alone."

Dan eased out of the seat and stood, his head bowed slightly because of the low ceiling. "I'm glad you're not alone, either," he replied with a sense of surprise. He would hate to think of her facing this danger on her own.

With a muffled sob she reached for him, her arms entwining around his waist. Dan wrapped his arms around her and held her close. He might have been irritated with her earlier in the day, but she *had* been trying to help him, even if he hadn't wanted her help.

She certainly didn't deserve this kind of treatment.

There was a slight commotion on deck which caught Dan's attention. Shannon straightened, but he didn't release her. One of the men opened the hatch and looked down at them.

"Ah, you're awake," he said with a smirk. "Good. It'll make it easier to get you on board. Come on, you two. We don't have all day for you to be playing kissy face."

Dan eased away from Shannon, then climbed up to the deck. He looked around to see where they were. There was no land in sight. One of the three men was already going up the ladder to the ship, while the other two waited impatiently. He glanced around and spotted another man at the wheel of the cabin cruiser. This must be their reluctant escort. Dan noticed that the man wouldn't look at him.

Without a word, he held out his hand to Shannon and helped her up to stand beside him.

The second man went up the ladder, and then Dan followed with Shannon right behind him. The last of the trio followed her up. As soon as they'd boarded the ship, the pilot of the boat gave a brief wave and headed back the way they had come.

When Dan reached the top and stepped on board he noticed that Shannon was shivering. The air had grown cooler as the sun dropped toward the west. He wrapped his arm around her shoulders and pulled her against his side. Of course she was afraid. He didn't blame her in the least. He wasn't feeling all that confident himself.

"Who the hell is this!"

He glanced up and saw a tall, well-built, silver-haired man striding toward them from the interior of the ship. Dressed in a silk shirt and dress pants, he exuded power and authority. Here was the boss man, no question about that.

Dan studied him as he drew closer, his face darkening with anger.

The leader of the three men said, "Sorry, Mr. Guardino, but it couldn't be helped. We was talking with the Doyle woman when this joker decided to butt in. Al had to knock some sense into him. We didn't wanna leave him there on the beach and since the lady insisted she knows nothing about Taylor, I figured we'd better bring 'em both, in case you wanted us to help jog her memory."

Guardino shook his head in disgust. "I can't believe

this. I send you on a simple errand and you turn it into a damned federal offense!''

Dan looked down at Shannon. She exchanged glances with him but didn't say anything. He wasn't certain whether they were worse off because Guardino's minions had overstepped their authority, or whether it might be the break they needed to be immediately returned to shore.

Guardino stopped in front of Dan and looked him over with curiosity. ''What's your name?''

''Dan Crenshaw.''

''Would you care to explain to me exactly how you're involved in all of this?'' he asked, doing little to mask his irritation.

Dan had been going over his options from the time he'd regained consciousness. There weren't all that many. He had to decide whether or not he believed Shannon. She might not be telling him everything she knew, but it was too late now to question her to make certain.

In the meantime, he wanted to make it clear that she was under his protection.

''I'm afraid I have no idea what's going on here. When I saw your men bothering my fiancée I attempted to stop them.''

He gave her shoulders a squeeze and smiled down at her as lovingly as possible given their present circumstances. He felt the jolt of his words go through her, but her expression remained the same.

Good girl.

''Your fiancée? Since when? I happen to know that she's Rick Taylor's girl.''

Shannon spoke up for the first time. ''That isn't true! I only dated Rick a few times. It was never anything serious.''

''That isn't the way *he* tells it.''

"I don't care *what* he says."

Dan figured it was time for him to speak. "Shannon and I grew up near the same small town. We've been a couple for years, except we had a fight a while back and she moved to St. Louis." He gave her another loving glance. "We kept in touch while she was away and I finally convinced her to give me another chance, so she moved back."

"Are you aware she was seeing Rick Taylor while she was in St. Louis?"

"She mentioned him in passing. That's all."

Guardino studied him in silence, then shook his head. "Let's get inside. The wind's coming up."

As soon as they entered the ship, Guardino told a crew member to find them some dry clothes and a place where they could change. Then he spun on his heel and walked away.

One of the men who had abducted them poked him in the back and said, "Okay, lover boy, let's go."

Dan would love nothing better than to throw the bastard off the side of the ship. In fact, he promised himself he'd make sure these jerks paid for this in some way. But at the moment he didn't want to do anything to put them in any more jeopardy.

He kept his arm wrapped around Shannon's shoulders as they followed a crewman down the hall. He paused in front of one of the doors, opened it, and cheerfully said, "Here you go, sir. Watch your head."

Dan stepped back and allowed Shannon to precede him into the room. He closed the door behind them. There were bunk beds in the room, plus a dresser, table and two chairs. He opened another door and spotted a lavatory, commode and what looked to be a miniscule shower.

Shannon wrapped her arms around her waist. "You

didn't have to make up that stuff about us getting married, you know. You could have pretended you'd never seen me before today. That wouldn't have been much more than the truth.''

''I know. I must still be playing Sir Galahad. I figured if they thought you had someone in your corner they'd treat you a little better. We can hope, anyway.''

''I've never been in a situation like this. I don't know what to do.''

''Cooperate,'' he replied. ''It's much safer that way.'' He went to the porthole and looked out. Nothing much to see. Water and more water. The sun was heading toward the horizon. ''I wish I knew what time it was.''

''I have no idea.''

''It was past noon when I saw you talking to those creeps. The sun sets around six o'clock this time of year. If that's true, then we must be several miles offshore.''

''I was so worried about you not waking up that I didn't pay any attention to anything else.''

He walked back to her. ''You have absolutely no idea why they're looking for this Rick person?''

''No.''

''How did you meet him?''

''Through a friend at work. We used to double date. Then she broke up with his friend, so Rick and I spent time together as a twosome. That's when I discovered that he has a gambling problem.''

''Ahhh, now we're getting somewhere.''

She looked at him in surprise. ''We are?''

''The dumb joker probably skipped out without paying a gambling debt.''

''I never thought about that.''

''Were you ever with him when he gambled?''

She nodded. ''He loved to go to the floating casinos

there on the river. He always insisted he never bet more than he could afford to lose. I've seen him make some big wins, but I sometimes wondered about his losses.''

''If he likes to gamble, you can bet he has other stakes in other places.'' He sat down on the edge of the lower bunk. ''They're going to want to know anything you know about the guy—his friends, his family, any names, phone numbers, anything that can help them find him.''

''But I've already told them that I didn't really know him that well. He was just somebody to go out with.''

He wished to hell his head would stop throbbing. ''Okay. So maybe they'll believe you and take us back to shore. But I have a strong suspicion it won't be tonight. Hope you don't mind having a roommate because I don't want them to separate us for any reason.''

''Thank you. I appreciate what you're doing for me.'' She smiled. ''Besides, I know I'm safe with you, Dan.''

She couldn't be that naive. Could she? There was absolutely nothing worse for a man's ego than to have a woman tell him she trusted him to behave as a gentleman.

Damn. He supposed he could live with it. He just hoped that Rafe didn't get wind of this little episode. Come to think of it, Rafe would be laughing his fool head off it he knew what had happened to him...again. This time Dan would have to come up with a way to get them out of this mess without outside help.

At least he didn't have to contend with a bullet wound this time around. Instead, he would be confined with a deliciously sexy woman and expected not to act on all the strong urges she'd awakened in him.

Another pain with which to contend.

How lucky could a guy get?

# Six

---

**D**an heard a tap on the door. He walked over and opened it. The crew member who had showed them to the room held out a small stack of clothing. "I'm afraid this was all I could come up with for you and the lady, sir. But at least they're dry."

"Thank you," Dan said, taking the clothing.

"I'll be waiting outside your cabin to show you to the lounge where Mr. Guardino is waiting to see you."

"All right." Dan closed the door and looked at the clothes. There was a long-sleeved dress shirt, a couple of T-shirts, and two pairs of denim jeans.

He held up the pants. There was no way they would fit Shannon. He turned to her and said, "I have a suggestion. The dress shirt looks big enough that it would almost be a dress on you. Why don't you step inside—" he motioned to the other room, "—and see what you think."

She took the shirt and disappeared behind the door.

While she was gone he peeled out of his bathing suit and grabbed the jeans. They were a little short and snug in the waist, but those were minor inconveniences. There was something about being almost bare that made any situation more uncomfortable—well, except for one... He removed the sweater and pulled on one of the T-shirts, thankful it was wide enough in the shoulders. Then he pulled the sweater back on. It seemed much cooler on the water than on shore.

Neither one of them had shoes, but it couldn't be helped.

The door to the head opened and he turned around. She looked like a little girl playing dress-up in Dad's dress shirt. She'd rolled the sleeves up to her elbows. The hem came almost to her knees.

"You look fine," he said.

She looked more than fine. It was funny how the mind worked. She'd revealed much more in her see-through jacket and two-piece suit. Now she was carefully buttoned up to the neck and looked sexy as hell.

Down, boy. This was not the time for him to be fantasizing about his companion.

He gave her what he hoped was a reassuring smile. "Are you ready to face our host? I have a hunch he's only just begun his interrogation of you."

She sighed. "I guess I don't have a choice. I hope I can convince him how little I know about Rick."

He held out his hand. "Come on. Maybe if we're docile enough, he'll take pity and feed us."

The crew member led them down one hallway and into another one before he paused and waved them into a large room, ornately decorated.

Dan realized that he wasn't too alarmed about the upcoming interview, despite the evidence that these people were capable of violence. He figured that Guardino was a businessman, pure and simple. Somebody owed him money, so he was leaning on whoever could help him collect. Once he figured out that Shannon didn't know anything about the deadbeat ex-boyfriend, their usefulness would end.

If Guardino were a sociopath, he'd toss them over the side. But from everything that Dan had picked up from their brief meeting, he didn't see Guardino as being that ruthless.

In which case, or so he devoutly hoped, Guardino would send them back to the island.

Guardino stood beside a bar that was fully equipped with any alcoholic beverage a person could want. A large tray of hors d'oeuvres sat on a nearby table. He spotted them and smiled. "Please. Come in and make yourself comfortable. What can I get you to drink?"

"Coffee sounds good to me," Dan said, sitting down and reaching for one of the hors d'oeuvres. Shannon looked at him, her surprise apparent.

What? He offered her a small cracker with all kinds of good stuff piled on top. She sat down beside him and took it. Before putting it in her mouth, she said, in a low voice, "Coffee?" and grinned at him, popping the morsel into her mouth.

That explained the look she'd given him. Well, hell. Surely she didn't think he'd start drinking in this situation?

"And you, Ms. Doyle?"

"Uh, actually, a glass of water would be great."

Guardino quirked an eyebrow. "Whatever you say." He turned away and picked up a crystal pitcher and deftly filled one of the glasses. He filled a cup with coffee and set the drinks on a tray, which he then carried to them.

He sat down across from them. "Let me introduce myself. I'm Gianni Guardino and I owe you both a tremendous apology. I can't imagine what my men thought they were going to accomplish by dragging the two of you back here."

Dan took another bite of the varied selection in front of him before picking up his coffee. Shannon helped herself to the food as well. It had been a long time since their shared breakfast, which seemed to have taken place in another life.

She took a sip from her glass of water, then faced Guardino. "Since you must have gone to a great deal of trouble to locate me, it's my guess they felt they were following your instructions, if only implicitly."

Dan continued to drink his coffee, refusing to look at either one of them. Her tone carried a hint of irritation, which he found amusing, given their uncertain circumstances. Frightened or not, she wasn't going to back down.

"To be honest, Ms. Doyle, when Taylor turned up missing we thought the two of you were together. We discovered that you had gone to Texas, that you had family there, so we thought he might be with you. We contacted your family and discovered your vacation plans." He eyed Dan with speculation. "Whoever it was we spoke to didn't mention a fiancé."

Shannon stiffened slightly. "You must have spoken to my grandmother."

"Yes, that's possible."

She glanced at Dan, then away. "She doesn't know about our engagement."

Dan patted her hand. "It's all right, darling. You can tell him the truth."

She looked at him with a hint of wariness. For good reason, of course.

"The truth is," he explained, "that her family really doesn't approve of me, which is why we decided to meet on the island and work out the details of our relationship before telling them we were back together."

Guardino sipped on his drink and appeared to be processing this new information. "Did they approve of Rick Taylor?" he asked after a few minutes.

Shannon sighed. "I was never serious about Rick. Therefore, my family knows nothing about him. We dated occasionally, that's all. I really don't know anything about him."

Guardino sat back in his chair and studied her for a lengthy moment before he murmured, "I'm disappointed to hear that." He drained his glass and set it down.

"I told your men that but they wouldn't believe me."

Another silence took over the room. Dan could hear the faint ticking of a clock. He glanced around and saw that it was almost five o'clock. It would be dark soon.

Guardino returned to the bar and made himself another drink. He waited until he sat down again before saying, "Well, Ms. Doyle, here's the way I'm looking at the situation. I figure that if you know where Rick is and he's asked you not to tell anyone, we would be hearing the same answer, don't you see? My men no doubt figured that it would be better to let me decide whether or not you were telling the truth."

Dan helped himself to the food as though the outcome of this conversation had nothing to do with him. The man was sharp, but Dan wasn't surprised. Guardino wouldn't be in the powerful position he obviously maintained without being a good judge of character.

"I guess the question that comes to mind, then," Dan drawled, "is whether or not you believe her?"

Guardino nodded thoughtfully. "Yes, that is the paramount question here. You see, Taylor's story is considerably different from yours, Ms. Doyle.''

"*His* story?" she repeated. "I don't understand."

"Rick is quite enamored of you. He spent much of his time bragging to all his friends about you, showing off photos, talking about a future with you." He glanced at Dan. "Obviously, he knew nothing of your—er—previous commitment to Mr. Crenshaw."

Dan shifted so that he faced her. "Why, Shannon. You led that poor man on out of some twisted need to get back at me? I am shocked and ashamed!"

She glared at Dan before turning to Guardino. "It wasn't like that at all. I didn't know he had photos of me, although he did take a camera along on one of our dates. Maybe he took some snapshots then, but I never gave him any indication that I considered him anything more than a friend."

"Were you seeing others at the same time?"

"Well, no. But I didn't date much while I was in St. Louis." She gave Dan a brief look as though he was the reason why.

"I understand that you held a technical consultant's position with a firm specializing in computers, is that correct?"

She nodded.

"And yet you gave up that position to return to Texas?"

"Yes."

Guardino studied her in silence for several moments. Dan decided it was time for him to speak up. "She was missing me, you see," he offered modestly. She gave him a withering look. He smiled at her in return, then leaned over and kissed her on the cheek. "I know. It's tough to swallow your pride and admit when you're wrong, but in the long run, it's worth it, don't you agree?''

Guardino made a sound of disgust, then asked, ''Did you ever meet any of Taylor's friends or family?''

''A friend. He was dating one of my co-workers. It was through them that I met Rick. Chad Harris, I believe his name is.''

''Mmm.'' Guardino went over to the bar and returned with the carafe of coffee to refill Dan's cup. ''Did he ever talk about his family?''

''Not that I recall.''

''Did he ever tell you what he did for a living?''

''He said he was into investments.''

''Investments,'' he repeated with disbelief. ''Really?'' Guardino shook his head. ''What an idiot,'' he muttered.

Dan spoke up. ''What does he do?''

''He used to work for me, calling on some of my customers. He just serviced accounts, made certain everything was running smoothly, collected payments.''

Dan kept his expression bland while his mind raced furiously. This wasn't about some gambling debt, although the guy's gambling habits might very well be behind it. Bright-boy Taylor must have been Guardino's bagman, collecting money on various racketeering activities. And he'd chosen to disappear without giving his boss his money. Obviously the man had a death wish.

Shannon asked, ''Did you check with Chad Harris, to see if he'd spoken to him?''

Guardino nodded. ''Chad finally managed to convince me that he didn't know a thing.''

There was something in the way the man said that which gave Dan pause. He wondered if Chad was still among the living and if so, how his health was these days?

All right, so now he was a great deal more worried than

he had been, but there still wasn't anything that he could see they could do about the situation except to ride it out.

Which was another thing. Was his queasiness due to his head injury or was the ride in this floating mansion getting a little rougher?

Just as he thought that, the bottles on the bar rattled and the room tilted slightly. Dan and Shannon grabbed for their drinks while Dan barely managed to stop the platter of food from sliding off the table.

In two strides Guardino was at the phone on the wall. With his back to the room, his conversation was muffled but his tone left it clear that somebody's head would be rolling for sloppy ship handling.

Dan took the opportunity to look at Shannon. He didn't like what he saw. Her fair skin was now pasty-white and her eyes seemed to fill her face. "Don't get sick on me now," he whispered.

"It's not that," she replied equally as soft. "Do you realize what Rick was doing?"

"Yeah, but I was hoping you didn't."

"He must have stolen money—"

"—to pay off gambling debts," Dan finished for her. "Boy, you know how to pick them, don't you?"

"I only dated him to help out a friend. It just became easier to go out with him than to keep making excuses why I couldn't."

"You worked for a computer company in St. Louis?"

"Yes."

"I don't suppose you happen to have a resume with you, by any chance. It just so happens that I'm in need of—"

"Very funny, Dan. Has anyone told you that your sense of humor needs a little work?"

Maybe it did, but at least his teasing had brought a hint

of color back into her cheeks. He still wasn't certain why she'd felt it necessary to barge into his life and start running it. That would be one of the first conversations they would have once they got back to shore. If she'd done it to get his attention, she'd certainly managed that, but, in general, he wouldn't recommend her tactics for a job applicant.

The sound of the phone slamming drew his attention back to their host, whose face had turned a mottled color. He'd hate to think what his blood pressure reading might be about now.

"The captain has just informed me," Guardino bit off as though taking a chunk out of each word, "that the tropical depression that has been playing around south of here has decided to move north, picking up steam as it goes. The Coast Guard has issued a warning to all vessels that we have a storm headed this way."

Dan nodded. "Well, we'd better put into shore. It shouldn't take long to get back to the island. Exactly how far out are we?"

"I have no intention of putting in anywhere along the Texas coast."

"Don't let our reputation disturb you," Dan replied genially. "We're all a pretty decent group of people, by and large. Maybe a bit arrogant at times, but that just goes with the territory."

"If I'm seen in this area, certain people will believe that I'm trying to solicit business. It isn't worth triggering a possible turf war. I've told the captain to get us to New Orleans as soon as possible."

"New Orleans!" Shannon jumped up. "But you can't! Don't you have a boat that could get us to shore?"

"Not in these heavy seas. I'm sorry, but you might as well make yourselves comfortable. You're going to be my guests for the next few days."

# Seven

$D$an stood. "I hope that you'll reconsider. Obviously, you had no trouble sending your three men to get us. They can see that we get back just as easily."

"I wish it were that simple. The seas are considerably rougher than they were earlier in the day. I'm not wasting time waiting around while you two get back to your pre-marital honeymoon. But I can assure you that you will have my ship at your disposal for the next few days."

"Dressed like this?" she said, looking down at the shirt that was successfully serving as a modest dress for her.

"Those were the most expedient items at the time. However, I will be happy to see what else we can find. We also have a much nicer stateroom for the two of you." He rubbed his hands together as though having successfully dealt with a knotty problem. "Now, then, dinner should be ready to be served in the dining room. Please follow me."

Guardino turned around and walked out of the room.

"Dan, what are we going to do? We can't stay on board!"

He walked over to one of the portholes and looked out. He flinched. The waves were rolling with a ferocity he'd never seen before. How could this thing have blown up so quickly?

He turned and said, "I'm not certain I'd want to be out in that in a smaller boat, Shannon. Come look."

He stepped back and allowed her to gaze out the opening. "Oh my God."

"I had the same reaction."

"How safe are we on this thing?"

"Darned if I know. I've never been one to get out on these babies. I'm much more comfortable on dry land."

"My sentiments exactly."

"You see, we've found something we can agree on. This is obviously a match made in heaven."

"This isn't funny."

"You will carefully note that I'm not laughing. I'm not even snickering. I don't like this situation any more than you, but there isn't a hell of a lot I can think of to do about it at the moment. And I'm still hungry. Since our host has offered to feed us, I say we should take him up on the offer."

He held out his arm to her as though to escort her to the dining room. She gave him a look that should have withered all his sensitive parts and marched past him without a word.

Women.

The puzzlement of mankind.

He was just trying to be polite.

* * *

Shannon couldn't believe it. Absolutely. Could. Not. Believe. It.

She was marooned on a yacht with Dan Crenshaw, posing as his fiancée. This had to be the single most humiliating thing that had ever happened to her.

When Mandy had told her of her concern about Dan she'd risked his reaction to her presence because she honestly thought that she could help him while easing Mandy's concern. Okay, and maybe she had hoped that he might find her attractive—show some interest in her. The very last thing she had ever intended was to be trapped in a pretend-type relationship. She'd never been so embarrassed.

And now they were going to share a stateroom?

Nothing was turning out the way she'd hoped and it was all her fault.

When she walked into the dining area she paused for a moment to appreciate the beauty of the room. No expense had been spared. She wondered where Mr. Guardino kept his yacht when he wasn't using it. Was its homeport in New Orleans? Were his headquarters in St. Louis?

She would dearly love to get her hands on Rick Taylor at the moment. She'd make darned sure he paid back every penny that he owed his boss before he drew many more breaths.

It was her association with him that had resulted in this whole mess.

Dan's sense of the ridiculous hadn't helped any.

Engaged?

Whatever had possessed him to mention an engagement? Why couldn't he have said they were friends? Now they were left to play out a farce that was becoming more uncomfortable by the hour.

"Please be seated," Guardino said to them when they

entered the room. "I've already sent instructions about your stateroom and was informed that my daughter left some of her clothing here the last time she was on board. I hope that you'll be able to find something that will make you more comfortable during your stay."

"Thank you," she said, sitting to his left. Dan took the chair across from her.

"Would you like wine with your meal?"

"No, thank you."

Dan shook his head.

They ate in almost complete silence. Shannon was exhausted. It had been a very long time since her early morning walk on the beach. It was difficult to imagine a more stressful day than this one.

All she wanted to do was to get some sleep.

As soon as she was finished, she asked to be excused. Guardino signaled for one of the attendants to show her where they would be staying during their journey.

The moment she saw the room, she knew she was in big trouble. There was only one bed. Although full sized, it was much too small to share with Dan, but her only other option was to ask to be alone or to sleep on the floor.

If Guardino were to think that they had lied to him about one thing, he might get it into his head that everything else they had told him was a lie. She didn't dare take the chance.

The bathroom, which she guessed was called a "head," was much larger in this suite. It was also furnished with soaps, shampoos and conditioners. She decided to help herself to the supplies by showering and washing her hair before she returned to the bedroom to look for clothes. If she'd understood him correctly, this was his daughter's room.

She started opening drawers. In one of the drawers she found lingerie, including panties, bras, slips and night-gowns.

When she lifted them to get a better look, she realized that she'd been thinking of a young, innocent schoolgirl. Whoever had left these was far from being a schoolgirl.

The sheer lace and satin items screamed seduction. She held up one of the bras and sighed with dismay. There was no way she could possibly fill that cup. She tossed everything back inside. She found another drawer filled with T-shirts, shorts and jeans, all of which were too large for her, but considerably more her size than her present apparel.

She pulled out one of the soft T-shirts. It would have to do for sleepwear because she refused to sleep in the same bed with Dan wearing one of those nightgowns. She returned to the lingerie drawer and reluctantly took out a pair of the panties, then returned to the bathroom where she changed into them.

The shirt reached her midthighs. Well, it couldn't be helped. The thought of wearing one of those see-through nightgowns made her shiver.

His daughter.

Hah.

Shannon returned to the bedroom and crawled into bed, moving as close to the wall as possible. She left the bed-side lamp on, pulled the covers up to her ears and turned her back to the room. Within minutes, she was asleep.

Dan leaned back in his chair and watched his solicitous host busy himself at the side table.

"I keep offering you choices for a drink. Are you an abstainer?"

Dan recalled his morning hangover and almost smiled.

"I'm taking it easy for a very simple reason. I haven't spent much of my time off dry land. I see no reason to add to possible problems. Particularly if the seas are going to continue to worsen."

Guardino smiled. "A smart man. You know your limits. Tell me, Dan, what sort of work are you in?"

"I'm retired at the moment."

"Really! You appear much too young for that. What were you doing before retirement?"

"I had a computer processing plant. We put together motherboards for specific orders."

"A good business to be in…it's continuing to expand as technology advances."

"That's my take on it, anyway," Dan replied.

"I could always use a good businessman in my organization. Perhaps we can come to a meeting of the minds while we're making our little journey together."

Dan smiled. "It's certainly something to kick around at another time. For now, though, I think I'm going to hit the sack." He rubbed his head. "This headache never did let up much."

Guardino pushed back from the table and stood. "You'll find pain relievers in your room, I'm sure. In the meantime, please let me apologize once again for the unnecessary roughness. I wouldn't want you to think that I run my business that way."

"Perish the thought." Dan, too, stood. "Is there someone who could show me where I'll be sleeping tonight?"

Guardino nodded. "With your fiancée, of course. I thought that was the least I could do since it appears that I interrupted a reconciliation."

*Oh, great. Just what I need. Well, I can always remind her of my headache.*

"I'll also go through my wardrobe to see if I can find

something that might fit you better. We seem to be of a similar size.''

''Thank you. I'd appreciate it.''

''Meanwhile, I'll have one of the crew show you to your room.''

Once in front of the door, Dan wasn't certain whether he should knock or just go inside. If Shannon was as tired as she'd appeared to be, she might be asleep. If so, he didn't want to disturb her. He hesitated, then quietly opened the door and peeked inside.

She'd left on a lamp beside the bed. If the small lump in the bed was any indication, she was sound asleep.

He tended to forget her lack of stature because she made such a large impression. Now he gazed at the bed and shook his head.

All he'd wanted was some time off, a chance to get away from his life. He distinctly remembered looking forward to peace. And quiet. Isolation. Downtime.

What had he done to merit all this attention? It seemed to Dan that the person really deserving of this harassment was Rick Taylor. Instead, he was an unwilling guest on a ship headed for New Orleans. A tropical storm was bearing down on them. His host, a man who used armed thugs to intimidate people, was offering him a job as if he should be flattered. And, if that wasn't bad enough, he now found himself sharing a bedroom with a young woman who had spent all of her time since he'd met her giving him a hard time.

Dan groaned.

The last thing he wanted to have to deal with was the complication of sharing a bedroom with Shannon Doyle. No matter how irritated he'd been with her since he'd awakened this morning, he'd found himself in a state of semi-arousal most of the time he'd been around her.

What did that say about him?

He hated to think.

Now, he was expected to share her bed. Yeah, right.

He looked around the room. Whoever decorated the place hadn't worried about the expense. He started to the head when he heard a soft tap on the door. Dan hurried over and opened it.

One of the ship's crew handed him a stack of clothing and walked away. Dan closed the door with his elbow and hip, then set the clothing down. Guardino had come through for him. There was underwear, and in his size at that; socks, a pair of sneakers, which looked to be close to his size, plus some khakis and pullover knit shirts.

He wondered if Shannon had lucked out as well.

No pajamas, though. Not that he'd ever owned a pair in his life. He bet Guardino didn't either.

Dan grabbed a pair of briefs and went into the head to take a shower. He also washed the stickiness out of his hair, being careful around the still swollen knots. He was pleased he hadn't seen anything more of those guys. Otherwise, he might have lost his affable demeanor in an effort to repay them.

He'd much prefer taking them out rather than playing this nonaggressive role. However, the personal satisfaction he would get wouldn't compensate for endangering their lives.

Dan dried off and pulled on the pair of briefs, then searched for the pain relievers. Once he found them, he took a couple and returned to the bedroom.

Shannon hadn't stirred. He carefully sat down on the side of the bed, turned off the light and slid between the sheets. Once horizontal, he was more aware than ever of the rough seas.

He could only hope that things would be better by morning.

# Eight

**A** particularly vicious jolt to the bed woke Dan some time later. He had no idea how long he'd been asleep but he could see from periodic lightning flashes that the storm was still out there. Now that he was awake, he could hear the steady pounding of rain.

He rolled from his side to his back and glanced over at Shannon. She was sitting up holding onto one of the brackets in the wall.

"Can't get much sleep in that position," he commented quietly.

"If I let go, I'm thrown against you."

"So? At least you won't be thrown out of bed." He patted the rail alongside the mattress. He held out his arm. "Come here."

Another flash of light revealed her face. She looked scared, even though her voice had sounded calm. She kept staring at him, then seemed to come to some decision because she slid back down into bed and allowed herself to roll against his side.

He lifted his arm so that she could rest her head on his shoulder. "That better?" he asked quietly.

"Much."

She had on some kind of cotton nightshirt, for which he was grateful. He wore nothing more than the borrowed underwear. He needed to concentrate on the storm and staying in bed, not on the fact that a very attractive woman was now snuggled up against him.

"So tell me, Ms. Doyle, exactly how did you get into this particular situation?" He pitched his voice to the soothing sound of a journalist doing an interview.

He felt more than heard her chuckle. "You've probably been asking yourself that very same question."

"Oh, but I know how I got here. In my effort to rescue the fair damsel, I got clobbered by the dragon. And you?"

"For trying to do a favor for a friend, I suppose."

"Which friend is that?"

She didn't answer right away. When she did, he got the impression she had changed her initial response. "When my co-worker in St. Louis begged me to go out on a blind date. Those things never work out."

"I see. And Taylor was the date."

"Yes."

"What made you decide to move to St. Louis in the first place?"

"I was fresh out of college and wanted to see a little more of the world than Texas. I received an offer to take a training position in a company there and thought it might be fun to move to St. Louis."

"Did you enjoy it?"

"Actually, I did. It was a five-hour drive to Chicago. Another five-hour drive to Memphis. I used to spend my weekends traveling. I went to Nashville one time, Louisville another time.''

''Alone?''

''Most of the time. Occasionally a female friend would agree to ride along, but usually they preferred staying in town with their boyfriends.''

''But not you.''

''I was enjoying my freedom too much.''

''Why don't I remember you? I recall Buddy, but I never knew he had a sister.''

''That isn't surprising. I'm five years younger than Buddy. I was going through that awkward stage by the time you were big man on campus. Very few people noticed me.''

''I find that really hard to believe.'' He was having a little trouble keeping his breathing even. She had shifted so that she was facing him. Her breasts rested against the side of his chest. Her breath felt warm against his throat, and her soft scent—a combination of flowers and herbs—teased all of his senses.

What had made him think he could lie next to her like this and not be affected? All right, so he was an idiot. What was he supposed to do at this point? Demand that she get back on her own side of the bed? The way the room was pitching, it was a wonder they both weren't thrown out of bed.

He started laughing.

''What's so funny?''

''I just tried to picture an amorous couple trying to accomplish anything in this kind of weather.''

He could feel her stiffen, then she relaxed and nodded. ''I suppose I should feel quite safe, then.''

''You mean you don't?''

"Well, no. Not exactly. I've never been in this situation before."

"Out to sea in a storm?"

"Well, that, too. I've—uh—never been in bed with a man before."

He was careful not to move, other than to ease his hip away from the padded side of the bed that was keeping him from falling out.

"Then it should be reassuring to you to know that even if I had designs on you, you don't have anything to worry about, given these conditions."

"I wouldn't have anything to worry about where you're concerned anyway."

"Oh? Any particular reason for you to think that?"

She shifted slightly and raised her head. "You sound offended."

"For your information, no man appreciates the idea that he's considered safe to be around."

"You're kidding, right?"

"Absolutely not."

"You just seemed to prefer being alone and made it clear my company wasn't needed or wanted."

"It wasn't you personally. I've had things on my mind and wanted to work through them on my own."

"Such as?"

"What I want to do with the rest of my life."

"Run your company, of course."

"Not necessarily. I'm thinking about selling it."

"Okay. So then what?"

"One thing for sure. I won't be making any plans to sail around the world."

She buried her face into his shoulder. After a moment, she said, "Don't you ever take anything seriously?"

"Now that's a good question. I'm afraid I've been taking myself a little too seriously lately. So maybe it was a good idea for you to decide to become my housekeeper.''

"Why, thank you. Now, you see? That wasn't so hard, was it? To admit that I might have done something right?''

He used the motion of the ship to turn toward her, which meant that she was plastered against him. "Of course, you get to pay for the fact that I wasn't ready to learn all of this.''

Dan touched her lips lightly, playfully with his. Despite the uncertainties that surrounded them, he felt better than he had in months.

Because of this woman—this irritating, captivating, tantalizing woman. Never had he felt so alive, nor so turned on. He reminded himself to keep this light.

Her tentative and shy response caught him off guard. She placed her fingers on his chest so delicately that he felt as though his skin had been touched by the wings of a butterfly. He brushed his mouth across her cheek, reveling in the silkiness of her skin, and was delighted when she moved her lips—ever so slightly—to come into contact with his once again.

With that tacit approval Dan relaxed and began to explore her pouty bottom lip, nipping at it, then carefully soothing it with his tongue. He also stroked her upper lip as well before he allowed himself to explore past her slightly parted mouth.

She sighed, her tongue greeting him, teasing him until he could scarcely breathe.

Dan eased away from her with a great deal of reluctance. "This could get dangerous,'' he muttered, pressing her head against his neck. He took several deep breaths before he said, "I shouldn't have done that but I'd be lying if I told you I was sorry.''

Her soft breath blew across his neck, causing chills to run over him. "We could always pretend we're necking in the back seat of the family car," she whispered.

"I would hope that we'd have on considerably more clothes, if that were the case."

As though his words were an invitation, Shannon ran her hand over his shoulder and down his back, causing him to shiver again.

"You *aren't* wearing much, are you?" she asked, amusement lacing the words.

"Uh, no. Our host loaned me some clothes but there weren't any pajamas in the stack."

"You should have seen what I found—see-through nightgowns of satin and lace. Makes you wonder how old his so-called daughter is."

"Oh, please, don't tease my imagination with that image, if you don't mind."

She paused at the waistband of his briefs, then slowly slid her fingers around the band until her hand was directly above his erection. "Oh, my, what have we here?" she whispered.

"You know damned well what that is, even if you've never been in bed with a man before!"

She lightly drew her fingers downward until she touched his hair-roughened thigh.

"Shannon," he said in warning. "You're going to set off an explosion that neither one of us will be able to control. Watch it."

Her light laughter echoed in the room. "You have no idea how safe I feel at the moment." She kissed him, her seductive mouth teasing and tormenting him, her tongue flickering over his until he took control of the kiss, drowning in her femininity.

With his last vestige of control, Dan sat up and allowed

the momentum of the ship's movement to propel him out of bed and across the room. The flickering lightning seemed to have moved away from them, leaving the room in heavy darkness.

"Dan?"

He couldn't see her, but he heard the concern in her voice.

"I can't do this, Shannon. I'm not a teenager with raging hormones who's willing to block out everything but the need of the moment. Were you telling me the truth when you said you've never made love before?"

The room was hushed and the tension stretched so tightly between them that he fully expected to hear the vibration.

"I—yes, that's true."

"And I have no protection with me. I can't deny how much I want to make love to you, but this whole situation we're in has put us in an untenable position. I've never been one to go in for casual sex and what I'm feeling right now is far from casual."

There was another long pause. The only light came from a couple of portholes, one near the bed, but too high to give him an indication of whether she was sitting up or lying down.

The motion of the ship kept him braced against the wall and he suddenly saw the ridiculousness of the situation. He was plastered against the wall like some shrinking virgin while she was in bed waiting for him to return.

As though following his thoughts, Shannon asked, "Do you think I'm trying to seduce you?"

"You don't have to try, honey, believe me. You are a walking, talking, breathing temptress that no man could ignore."

She didn't say anything.

He wished he could see her face, wished he knew what she was thinking. He felt like an absolute fool and there wasn't a thing he could think of to do to relieve the tension of their situation.

Shannon knelt in the middle of the bed, grateful for the lack of light in the room. Now, for the first time, she understood what all the hoorah was about sex.

She'd never been so turned on in all her life. All she really wanted to do at the moment was to wrap herself around Dan Crenshaw and stroke every inch of his gorgeously delectable body.

My God. Had she completely lost her mind?

Forget her adolescent crush on the man for a moment, even if she had just met him for the first time two days ago, she would have reacted in the same way to being in bed with him. Add to that all the fantasies her fevered imagination had come up with over all these years, with each fantasy male wearing Dan's face, and she knew without a shadow of a doubt that she was in deep trouble.

The problem was that she had never been aroused by a man before. In fact, she had found their groping hands and sloppy kisses distasteful. When Dan had grabbed and kissed her that first night before immediately passing out, she'd ignored her strong reaction by putting it down to nerves. After all, she'd never done anything close to picking up a man in a bar before and taking him home.

What was she going to do?

She was glad she'd told Dan that she hadn't been with anyone else. She wanted him to know that she didn't sleep around. From her recent behavior with him, she could certainly see where he might have gotten a different impression of her.

"I feel as though I owe you an apology," she finally said into the darkness.

"An apology! For what?"

She thought about that for a while. "Well, if I had more experience, I would better understand what's going on here—what you're going through. For that matter, I'd understand what *I'm* going through." At the moment her skin seemed to ripple with sensation. She felt hot and cold at the same time. Not sure if she wanted to laugh or to cry.

"Look, this was my fault, okay? I should never have said anything about being engaged. It was a dumb idea and if I'd given it more thought, I would never have done it. But the fact remains that until we're off this ship, we're going to have to at least pretend to be lovers."

"Okay."

"Which means we're going to have to share that blasted bed."

She waited, but when he didn't speak, she said, "Okay."

"I must have been out of my mind to think that I could have you lie next to me and not be affected."

"I was affected, too."

He groaned. "I could have gone all night without that little admission, but thanks for sharing."

"I think you're making too much of this, Dan. It's perfectly normal for two healthy adults who are attracted to each other to want to make love. Isn't that one of our basic instincts?"

"Oh yeah. Very basic. I suppose I've been under the impression that I could control my oh-so-basic instincts and behave like a civilized male. Until recently, that is."

In a very quiet voice, Shannon said, "You did, Dan.

That's why you're somewhere across the room from me right now.''

She heard his gusty groan clear across the dark cabin. ''The distance between us at the moment is all that's keeping me from making hot, passionate love to you, Ms. Doyle.''

She smiled and wrapped her arms around her waist. He made it sound like a threat. She saw it as more of a promise.

# Nine

When Shannon woke up the next morning, she was alone.

Dan had dressed and left their room after their discussion the night before. If he had come back some time during the night, she hadn't heard him.

She had no idea what time it was, but from what she could see, heavy rain clouds covered any sign of the sun. It could be dawn or noon or somewhere in between.

She looked into the closet and was relieved to find some slacks and long-sleeved shirts hanging there. She wouldn't have been surprised if she had found slinky cocktail dresses.

The clothes were still a few sizes too large for her, but that didn't matter. One of the pairs of slacks had a belt, which she was able to tighten. The sleeves, once rolled, were fine.

After Shannon finished dressing, she went in search of breakfast.

The dining room was empty but she heard voices coming from the lounge. She peered around the opening and saw Guardino and Dan standing at the portholes, talking and drinking coffee from large mugs.

She spotted the coffee carafe on the bar and headed toward it, praying they had left her some.

"Good morning, Ms. Doyle," Guardino said as soon as she stepped through the door. "I hope you slept well."

She gave a quick glance at Dan, who hadn't shaved. His hair looked as though he'd been running his fingers through it, and his khakis looked rumpled.

The beachcomber look was back.

"Quite well," she said, which was somewhat the truth. It had taken her forever to get back to sleep once Dan left, but when she finally managed to drift off she'd gone out like a light.

Once again her eyes sought out Dan who looked away from her, then lifted his mug to his mouth.

She turned from him and poured herself some coffee.

Guardino said, "I've checked with the captain, who says the storm may be lessening. The weather service says it looks like the tropical storm has stalled on its way north."

"That's reassuring," she replied, taking her coffee over to the long sofa, where she sat down.

"You know," Dan said quietly from somewhere behind her, "I've been thinking. There's no reason for you to take us to New Orleans. You could drop us off in Galveston, which won't be out of your way. In fact, there would be no reason for you to go ashore. Just have one of your crew take us in on one of your launches."

"If I didn't know better, I'd think you don't care for my hospitality," Guardino replied.

Dan walked around the sofa and sat down at the opposite end from Shannon. "We weren't given any choice in the matter, as you know. We have families who will worry when they don't hear from us."

"Do you intend to tell them where you've been?"

Shannon gave Dan a sharp glance, but his expression wasn't giving anything away.

"There's no reason to, given the fact we've been gone less than twenty-four hours."

"How do you intend to get back from Galveston?"

Dan smiled. "I figured you'd give us enough money to rent a car. There's no reason to make the situation any worse by prolonging it."

"I'll check with the captain, and see how long it will take to get to Galveston. I think you may have come up with a solution that will satisfy everyone."

After a brief conversation by phone with the bridge, Guardino hung up and said, "Are you ready for breakfast?"

When Dan didn't say anything, Shannon stood and said, "That sounds wonderful."

The three of them were served their meal in the dining area. No one spoke until the table had been cleared.

"By the way," Guardino said, "I notice you aren't wearing an engagement ring. Why not?"

Oh, lordy, she hadn't given that detail any thought. This would not be a good time to let their host know they'd been lying to him, but her mind was blank.

Once again, Dan saved the day. "Actually, I'm giving her my mother's engagement ring. It's currently being resized. We're to pick it up when we return to Austin."

"I see. And when do you expect to do that?"

"Well, I need to get back to the island to handle some details there. Then we'll probably head north."

"Is there a date set for the wedding?"

Dan looked at her as though throwing her the conversational ball.

Shannon said, "We—uh—we're discussing it. It's hard to decide until we check with family and friends."

"But it will be soon, I hope?" Guardino asked.

"Soon?" she repeated.

"I really don't approve of the modern way of doing things—living together before marriage. That sort of thing. I made certain my daughter was a virgin when she walked down that aisle. She was a little put out by my insistence on certain things, but she has since thanked me." He smiled. "She and her husband are expecting their first child next spring. As a matter of fact, they honeymooned right here on this yacht last summer."

*Oh my gosh, these clothes really are his daughter's.*

The phone buzzed and he answered it. When he hung up, Guardino smiled at them and said, "It looks like you two are in luck. The captain said we can be in Galveston in a couple of hours." He looked at Dan. "I can't tell you how much I appreciate how you've handled this matter, Dan—I hope I can call you that. I feel that I've gotten a good indication of what kind of man you are." He glanced at Shannon. "Perhaps a bit impetuous, but I can understand your fear of losing her after all she's put you through."

Shannon raised her brows.

He explained, "Moving away really doesn't resolve anything. I hope you've learned that you have to stay and face your problems."

"Oh. Well, yes, I agree."

"You shouldn't have gotten mixed up with Rick Taylor. He's developed some bad work habits."

"Uh, yes, I suppose he has if you're looking for him."

"Oh, I'll find him. I needed a little vacation time, so this hasn't been a wasted trip. I hope you'll forgive me for interrupting your time together."

She nodded, not sure what to say. Dan sat watching them with little expression. Shannon said, "If you'll excuse me, I'll see about figuring what to wear once we reach Galveston."

Guardino waved his hand and said, "Oh, don't worry about it. My daughter will never miss any of her things. Help yourself." He turned to Dan. "You, too. It's the least I can do. Oh! That reminds me." He reached into his back pocket and pulled out his wallet. "This should get you back to your place with no problem."

He handed the money to Dan. Shannon tried not to stare. There were several bills—all of them hundreds.

Dan took them. "Thank you."

Then Guardino pressed a slip of paper into Dan's hand. "Go to this car rental establishment. I know you have no credit card, no identification, but this place will rent you a car, I assure you. I've also had one of the crew members put shaving gear in your room."

Dan rubbed his jaw and smiled. "Thank you again."

"Now, then, if the two of you will excuse me, I have some business to take care of. If I don't see you again, I wish you a pleasant journey back to the island."

Dan followed Shannon back to their room. As soon as they were inside, she asked, "What do you suppose that's all about?"

"He had a decision to make where we were concerned. He's decided we aren't going to give him any trouble over this and he's absolutely right."

"Why did he give you so much money?"

"Who knows? It probably isn't all that much to him. Did you enjoy the lecture on anticipating your wedding vows?"

"Well, actually, I agree with him. Not that I've ever given much thought to getting married, but I think the risks are too great to be careless."

"Glad to hear that. I got the impression that I had disappointed you last night."

She could feel herself turning red. "Not at all," she replied in a stifled voice.

"Had we had protection, I'm not at all sure I would have been so noble, regardless of your views on chastity."

She grinned. "I'm glad one of us had a hint of sanity left. I can admit to you now that I was a little carried away."

"Really? I would never have guessed." He rubbed his jaw. "Between you and Guardino, you're going to turn me into a presentable human being after all."

"I never told you to shave."

"Not in so many words. Your eyes speak volumes."

"Really?"

"Such as now," he said, moving closer to her.

"Oh?" She tilted her head back so that she could keep eye contact. "Exactly what are they saying?"

He grinned and slid his arms around her, drawing her close. "That you truly appreciate my restraint, within reason."

His kiss was anything but tentative. It was as if he'd been saving up all the intensity they had felt the night before, unleashing it now.

The last thought Shannon had before she gave herself up to the moment was that from now on, she'd better guard what her eyes were telling him; it seemed they couldn't keep a secret.

It was close to one o'clock when the launch arrived at the landing dock in Galveston. Rain continued to fall in sheets as the wind pushed it inland. Although they had not seen Guardino after they returned to their room, he had sent them weatherproof jackets with hoods.

Now that they were on dry land, Dan had cause to be grateful. He looked up and down the street. Not much traffic in this weather in off-season. He glanced down at Shannon. All he could see was her nose barely showing from the hood.

"You okay?" he asked, trying to block the wind from her.

"I've been better," she admitted. "What are we going to do now?"

"Look for a cab, I suppose. I don't even have change to make a phone call. Maybe we'd better look for a bank—or someplace where we can get change for one of these bills."

"I can't believe he actually turned us loose."

He laughed. "You know, our trouble is we've watched too many movies about guys like him. He has his own code of ethics, but you can't really blame him for wanting to get his money back from Rick."

"But can you imagine going to so much trouble to find me? To call my family and actually chase me all the way to the beach? Now that's scary."

They continued to walk as they talked. Dan spotted a restaurant in the next block. "Let's get something to eat. They'll take our money, I'm sure."

"We look like a couple of drowned rats," she said, glancing up at him, then away.

She was trying to walk in sneakers that were several sizes too large for her, but were better than being barefoot. By the time they reached the restaurant, Dan was more than willing to find a dry place to spend some time.

They removed their coats and hung them inside the door, then followed the hostess to one of the back booths.

The waitress showed up with coffee. They both nodded and ordered a sandwich apiece. When she left, they drank the coffee without speaking.

Finally, Dan said, "You know, Shannon, if I have to be abducted, I'm glad it was with you. Despite being frightened, you handled yourself very well."

She'd been cupping her hands around the hot coffee mug when he spoke. She glanced at him with surprise.

"A compliment? From you? I'm speechless."

He grinned. "That will be the day. All I'm saying is that things could have been much worse. But we're safe now."

"Safe but several hours away from our cars."

"Guess we can't have everything."

The waitress returned with their sandwiches and once again they were silent. When she was finished eating, Shannon settled back in the booth with a sigh of contentment. "I'll be glad to get out of these wet jeans, but I'm thankful I'm not still wearing my bathing suit."

"I'll guarantee you would have gotten all kinds of attention in that outfit."

"You've been a very good sport about all of this," she said. "I wouldn't have guessed you would be this calm from the mood you were in yesterday."

"Nothing like facing the fact you might not survive a kidnapping to get you to thinking."

"Is that what you've been doing?"

"Yeah. I've been counting my blessings and discovered

that I have a great many things to be thankful for that I had somehow overlooked during the past few months.'' He took her hand. ''I would like to get to know you better. I'm hoping that, once we get back to Austin, we can spend some time together.''

She smiled at him. ''I'd like that.''

Feeling lighter than he had in months, Dan returned her smile. ''Me, too.'' He looked at the wall clock nearby and said, ''We've got a seven-hour drive ahead of us, and from the looks of the weather, it'll be raining all the way. I guess we need to get started.''

When he paid for their lunch, he asked the hostess if she would mind calling a cab for them. When it arrived, they gave the driver the address Guardino had provided.

Once they filled out the paperwork and left the island, Shannon curled up on her side of the car and went to sleep.

Dan turned on the radio to keep him company. He had a lot to think about, anyway.

Maybe he'd give Rafe a call in the morning, just to get a feel for what was happening at the company. If there were no dire emergencies, he was thinking about staying on at the island for a few days. He'd see if Shannon would like to stay. After all, she *had* volunteered to be his house-keeper.

He was hoping that she might decide to be more than that. The next time he found her in an amorous mood, he'd make damn sure he was prepared to protect her.

Dan set the cruise control and settled back, humming along with the radio.

# Ten

It was after midnight when they walked into the condo on South Padre Island.

"It's hard to believe that we've only been away from here a little more than twenty-four hours," Shannon said, pausing in the living room and looking around. "A lot has happened in that time."

Dan paused by the wet bar as was his habit before he realized that he had no desire for a drink.

The drive had been long and he was tired, but sleep sounded better to him than alcohol.

He walked over to her and said, "We've had a busy couple of days. Let's hit the sack. Tomorrow I'd like to talk to you about staying here for a few days." He made a point not to touch her. "Maybe start all over. I promise not to yell at you for getting me up early."

She tilted her head back and studied him. "You don't

look so bad for a guy who's been hit on the head and dragged away for a forced sea voyage.''

"Actually, you don't look any worse for wear, either, although I would guess that you're going to enjoy wearing shoes that fit.''

Shannon laughed. "You're right.'' She stepped back, as though aware of the sexual tension that had sprung up between them. "So. I'll see you in the morning. Maybe not for a dawn walk, though. We could both use some rest.''

Dan followed her down the hallway and went into his room. He hadn't had but a few hours sleep since he'd left the condo. After getting dressed the night before, he'd gone to the lounge and attempted to nap on the sofa. He hadn't trusted himself to sleep in the same bed with Shannon without making love to her.

The thought bothered him. He was feeling downright lecherous where she was concerned. It wasn't that he just wanted to make love to her. He wanted more—to spend time with her, to watch her in the kitchen, listen to her laugh, feel her close to him at night.

He stripped and crawled into bed, basking in the comfort of having plenty of room. He stared at the ceiling, his hands behind his head, thinking about all that had transpired.

If he didn't know better, he'd think he was in love.

Of course, that wasn't possible.

His life was in shambles. He didn't have time for a relationship, even a casual one. Regardless of what else might be happening, he knew his feelings were far from casual where Shannon was concerned.

He was too tired to be trying to solve the question of his relationship with her tonight. He rolled over and closed his eyes, smiling at the thought that she would be the first person he saw in the morning.

The next thing Dan knew, he was awakened by the sound of heavy pounding somewhere nearby. He sat up, trying to get his bearings. His bedside clock registered six o'clock.

What was going on? It was still dark outside.

The pounding continued and he realized it came from his front door. Thinking there was an emergency, Dan leaped out of bed, grabbed a pair of jeans and after hurriedly pulling them on, raced to the front door. He pulled it open and stared in blank surprise.

A burly stranger—several inches taller and considerably wider than Dan—faced him with a ferocious glare. "Where the hell is she?"

"Huh?" Dan shoved his hair off his face, then finished zipping his jeans, trying to make some sense out of what was happening.

"Are you going to deny that you've got her here?" the stranger—who seemed vaguely familiar to Dan—belligerently asked.

This was no way to be awakened first thing in the morning. Dan put his hands on his hips and demanded, "What are you talking about? Who the hell are you?"

Just as he said it, he suddenly realized who he was talking to—this was Buddy Doyle, Shannon's brother. Her very large brother. Her very angry brother. And for some unknown reason, he appeared to be angry with Dan.

Buddy started to speak, then glanced over Dan's shoulder. Dan turned his head and spotted Shannon behind him.

"Buddy, what are you doing here?" she asked, sounding incredulous.

Dan turned back to Buddy just as Buddy caught him with a strong upper cut against his jaw, which sent Dan flying backwards, eventually landing on his butt in the middle of the living room floor.

Buddy followed him inside and slammed the door behind him. "You might think you're too damned important to show respect to us lesser beings, Crenshaw," Buddy was saying through the ringing in Dan's ears, "But you're not getting away with this."

"Buddy!" Shannon cried, rushing to kneel beside Dan. "What's gotten into you! Have you lost your mind?" Dan was vaguely aware that Shannon wore some kind of nightshirt that barely reached to midthigh.

"More to the point, Shannon," Buddy replied in a deep growl, "I want to know what—or who—has caused you to lose all sense of decency."

Dan carefully felt his jaw to make sure it wasn't broken while Shannon worriedly patted him.

Dan shoved her hand aside. "You've got it all wrong, Buddy," he began, mumbling his words. His jaw felt numb, but he had a hunch feeling would be returning any moment now.

"Oh, yeah?" Buddy asked. "You gonna look me in the eye and swear you haven't slept with her?"

Dan closed his eyes and rubbed his forehead, trying to gather his thoughts into some kind of order.

Shannon jumped up and faced her brother. "Buddy, it is absolutely none of your business what I do," she said with righteous indignation. "I'm almost thirty years old, for Pete's sake. I don't need a keeper."

"If this bastard has slept with you, then you're going to have more than a keeper. You've just acquired a soon-to-be-husband." He glared at Dan who had chosen to remain seated on the floor while the Doyles continued their spirited family discussion. He didn't need any more reminders of Buddy's legendary strength.

Buddy hadn't taken his eyes off Dan. "Just tell me you haven't slept with her and I'll apologize for jumping to conclusions about this situation—" he looked around the room, then at Shannon's skimpy attire before adding "—and take her home with me."

"Well, actually," he began—trying to figure out how to explain to an angry brother the difference between sharing a bed with a woman and... He wasn't given the chance.

"Did you sleep with her?" Buddy demanded.

Dan tried his most reasonable tone of voice. "We shared a bed, yes. But we didn't—"

"Don't start trying to bring up technicalities about what does and does not constitute a sexual relationship. All I need to know is that you were in bed together. You've confirmed it. Thank you." He turned to Shannon. "Go get your things and let's go. We've got a wedding to plan."

"Buddy," Shannon yelled, "You are not going to dictate how I live my life, do you hear me?"

"Oh, I'm not dictating anything."

"That's good to hear," she replied with sarcasm.

"I'm just following Grandma's instructions," he stated with a grim expression on his face.

"Grandmother?" she repeated weakly.

"Yep."

"She sent you down here?"

"Yep." He folded his arms across his massive chest. And smiled. With sudden good humor.

"Oh my," she said and turned away.

Now that Buddy was looking less ferocious, Dan decided he could safely get to his feet. He wasn't sure what to rub first, his jaw—which had come out of numbness with a vengeance—or his sore butt, which must be sporting a hell of a bruise from his sudden forced landing on the floor.

"Button your damned jeans," Buddy growled.

Dan became aware of how all of this must look to Buddy. He stood there wearing nothing but zipped, unbuttoned jeans, while Shannon wore a short nightshirt. He buttoned his jeans and shoved his hair out of his face once again. "I need some coffee. You want some?" he said over his shoulder to Buddy on the way to the kitchen.

"Sure, if you've got any."

Buddy ambled behind him like a grizzly bear checking out new territory. Dan glanced at Shannon and muttered, "Go get some clothes on," as he strode past her.

She looked as though she wanted to argue, but after a quick glance at her brother, she seemed to change her mind and disappeared down the hallway that led to the bedrooms.

Dan made coffee without saying anything to Buddy.

"Great place you have here," Buddy commented after several minutes of prowling from window to window in the living room.

"Thanks."

"Hope there's no hard feelings," Buddy genially said. "Now that we're going to be related, I don't figure we should be enemies or anything."

Dan rubbed his jaw again. That was a statement Dan could definitely agree with. He in no way wanted to be on Buddy's enemy list.

He poured the coffee and carried oversized mugs into the living room. He handed one to Buddy before carefully lowering himself onto his softly padded recliner. He nodded to the couch and watched as Buddy sat down across the room from him.

"Thanks," Buddy said a little sheepishly.

Dan stared out the wall of glass that faced east. The sky was slowly lightening. He ignored the man on the couch while he sipped his coffee.

Okay, so he was being rude. He didn't figure he was in a contest with his former teammate on that score. Buddy had won, hands down.

As the clouds on the horizon began to turn pastel shades of color, Buddy quietly said, "Wow. What a view."

Dan didn't reply. He had finished his coffee and was contemplating whether he wanted to stir himself to go get another one when Buddy finally said in an apologetic tone, "She's my only sister."

Dan could think of nothing to add to that statement.

"I couldn't stand the idea that you were taking advantage of the crush she used to have on you."

Dan slowly turned his head and stared at Buddy. "What are you talking about?"

"Aw, you must have known about it back when we were in school. She used to come to all the football practices, as well as every game, just so she could watch your every move. She collected any discarded photos taken of you by the yearbook staff, clipped them from the local paper, even took some of you around school. Her room was full of them. It broke her heart when you went off to that fancy eastern college."

"Are you by any chance talking about Shannon?" Dan asked politely.

"Of course I'm talking about Shannon! Who the hell did you think?"

Dan stared at him for several minutes before he said, "I never even knew your sister when I was in school."

Buddy didn't say anything.

Dan watched the sun peek above the horizon.

"You didn't know about her crush?" Buddy finally asked.

"Nope."

After another long pause, Buddy said, "Then don't tell her I told you about it, okay?"

Oh, sure. Like Dan would want to mention anything of that nature to Shannon. However, the idea did intrigue him. Hell, that was almost twenty years ago. She'd been a kid. Surely she'd gotten over an adolescent crush years ago.

She'd never been to bed with a guy before, he reminded himself. That had to count for something. And she had not pushed him away when he'd shown definite signs of wanting to make love to her that night on the yacht.

In fact, he'd known without a doubt that she would have allowed him to make love to her despite her virginal state.

Now why was that? he wondered.

Buddy's comments had set him to thinking—about several things.

"You know," Dan said after a few minutes, "I think I'd like to meet this grandmother of yours."

Buddy nodded. "That can certainly be arranged."

Dan discovered that his mood had lightened along with the sky. He smiled for the first time since he'd awakened this morning. "How about another cup of coffee, Buddy?" he said, standing and stretching. "I bet we could coax Shannon into making us a big breakfast if we ask nicely."

Buddy looked at him in surprise. He, too, stood. "Another cup of coffee sounds good. So does breakfast."

Dan returned to the kitchen and poured more coffee. "Have a seat, and I'll go see what's holding up Shannon."

He tapped on her bedroom door. After a long pause, he finally heard her say, "Come in."

He opened the door and stepped inside, closing the door behind him. Shannon sat on the side of her bed. She didn't look at him. Instead, she kept her eyes trained on her hands, clasped in her lap. She was now completely dressed in a brightly colored sundress he hadn't seen before. Her hair was pulled back from her face in a dignified knot at the nape of her neck.

"Shannon?"

She reluctantly lifted her head and gazed at him, wincing when she got sight of his swollen jaw. She went back to studying her hands. "It seems that all I do around you is apologize." Her dark eyes glistened and he realized that she'd been crying.

"The only thing damaged was my dignity," he replied lightly. "I'm sure I'll recover."

"I can't believe Buddy would come barging in like that," she said. Without looking at him, but with a firmer resolve in her voice, she added, "The sooner I get out of your life, the better."

Dan leaned his shoulder against the door and folded his arms across his chest. "That's going to be a little difficult, given the circumstances."

She jerked her head up. "What circumstances?"

"Why, Shannon, honey," he drawled. "You and I are going to be taking part in a family wedding real soon. If you're planning on a formal gathering, I'd suggest you have your brother carry a white shotgun."

# Eleven

——

"**D**on't be ridiculous," she said, coming off the bed like she'd been shot out of a cannon.

"Yeah, this isn't exactly the way I saw myself getting married, either," he replied with a shrug. He straightened. "Under the circumstances, I think you'd better plan to go back home today, after all. I'm sure there's all kinds of plans to be discussed with your family." He opened the door. "Oh, before you leave, would you mind fixin' us some breakfast, sugar?"

He closed the door before the shoe she'd picked up could connect with his head. He heard it bounce off the door. Yep, she had a temper. He was sort of looking forward to the taming of Shannon.

When he walked back into the kitchen, Buddy eyed him suspiciously. "That took you long enough."

"I'm not real sure how to break the news to you, my friend, but Shannon is not taking our newly engaged status real well. It looks like I'm going to be feeding us if we plan to eat."

"You know how to cook?" Buddy asked hopefully.

"I can fry bacon and make toast. The eggs might be a problem. Maybe scrambled will work."

"Sounds good to me. So what's been happening with you since the last time I saw you?"

What was it with those two? Shannon wondered, throwing her clothes into her bag. Or was it men in general? Did they actually expect her to marry Dan just because— she paused and looked around. Why *would* Dan take Buddy's threats seriously, anyway? He knew very well that nothing had happened between them.

It was obvious that she would have to have a long talk with her grandmother as soon as possible. At least she could have a rational conversation with *her*.

Shannon had no intention of getting married any time soon…and when she did decide to marry, she would certainly have a choice about who the bridegroom would be.

It would not be Dan Crenshaw.

That was when her conscience decided to show up to discuss the matter. Just what she needed.

*You were willing to make love with him but you won't marry him? Care to explain that one to me?*

"I was carried away by the moment, that's all. Once I had the opportunity to think about it, I knew that Dan and I would never work as a couple."

*Oh, you did. And when did you discover this new information?*

"It was a childish crush, that's all it was. His eyes enamored me. Very few people have those dark blue— almost pansy-colored—eyes."

*Honey, there's nothing pansylike about that man and you know it.*

"Cute. Real cute. The point is that Dan and I don't love each other. I've always known that I would not marry until I knew beyond any doubt that I loved a man and that he loved and was devoted to me."

*Well, give him a chance. Wasn't that what you wanted when you came looking for him? Didn't he mention that he wanted to spend more time with you? You came down here hoping for a chance to get to know him better, as well as a chance for him to find out more about you, right? That's what engagements are for, you know. A chance to plan your future.*

"I am not engaged."

She heard another tap on the door and immediately flushed before she realized that her muttering couldn't possibly have been heard. "Yes?" she answered calmly.

The door opened and a grinning Dan stuck his head around it. "Breakfast is ready." The door immediately closed. She heard him humming as he returned down the hallway.

Dan? Grinning? Humming?

Well, that explained it. The blow to his head had short-circuited something in his brain. She would go have a talk with her brother and make both men realize that this wasn't some silly game to be discussed and decided between the two of them.

Maybe she could knock both their heads together. That would probably be a real improvement.

Shannon did a last check of the area, picked up her bag and left the room. She smelled burned bacon as soon as she stepped into the hallway. Well, at least they hadn't waited for her to come feed them. They were obviously smarter than they appeared to be.

She set her bag beside the front door, then went in search of coffee. As soon as she stepped into the kitchen the men stopped talking and turned to look at her. Darned if each of them didn't have a distinctly guilty expression on his face. What, exactly, were they up to?

"Mornin'," Buddy said sheepishly. "It's good to see you again, Shannon."

She ignored him and poured her coffee before she turned around and leaned against the cabinet.

"Care for some breakfast?" Dan asked, waving his hand over the dubious collection of burnt toast, charred bacon and the unappetizing sight of undercooked scrambled eggs.

She gave him her ultimate fake smile and said, "I think I'll pass."

He looked disappointed.

Too bad.

"Uh, Shannon," Buddy said, "I'm sorry if I came on a little strong earlier."

"A *little* strong? You were totally out of line and you know it."

"Well, Dan understands. He has a sister, too, you know. It's hard not to be protective."

She finished her coffee and set the cup in the sink. She turned back and looked at her brother, a man that she usually admired. But not this morning. "Try," she said and walked out of the room.

She was already at the elevator when Dan came dashing out of the apartment.

"Where are you going!" he demanded.

Where was the elevator when you needed it? "Home," she said, staring at the button she'd pushed, willing the response time to be minimal.

"You can't leave yet. We've got to discuss a few things before you go home."

Ah. She heard the rattle of her means of escape. "Actually, Dan, we have absolutely nothing to discuss. You can stay here for the rest of your life, as far as I'm concerned. Your business can go into bankruptcy. I don't care. I should never have barged into your life in the first place. It was behavior that was totally out of character for me and I have paid for my mistake." The doors opened and she stepped inside. "Goodbye, Dan. Have a nice life."

The doors closed, leaving him standing there with his jaw—his swollen jaw—hanging open.

Dan sat at his usual table in the bar that night, nursing his Scotch. He'd been sipping on the thing for the last three hours.

Not much had changed in the place. Of course he'd only missed being there a couple of nights. What had he expected?

He supposed that what he had expected was that everything around him would have changed in the same way he had in that period of time.

The truth was, he felt lost at the moment. How could he have gotten so used to having Shannon in his life so fast? Someone he hadn't wanted around in the first place? Someone who was a real pain in the butt most of the time?

He didn't know, but that's what had happened.

Hell, he might as well go back to work. He certainly wasn't going to be happy sitting around here. He finished his drink and stood, walked over to the bar and said to Laramie, "Sorry about leaving so abruptly the other night. What do I owe you?"

Laramie laughed and told him the amount of his tab.

"Can't say I blame you for forgetting everything but your new friend."

He shook his head. "Not new. We've known each other for years." Well, it wasn't exactly a lie, just because he didn't remember her.

"Lucky you."

"Yeah," Dan replied, pocketing his change and walking out the door. "Lucky me."

The following afternoon Dan paused at the gate of the C Bar C Ranch, tapped in the numeric code that opened the gate, entered the ranch and officially returned to his world.

The black-topped road he followed wound through the hills dotted with centuries-old live oak trees. Longhorn cattle grazed in a few of the pastures he passed. Others held sheep and goats.

A windmill lazily spun in the breeze, pumping water into a holding tank.

Caleb Crenshaw had settled there more than fifty years ago. Dan wondered if his grandfather would have believed they could continue it as a working ranch this long.

Dan knew he couldn't have done it without help. Before his father died, he'd hired Tom Parker to manage the ranch. Tom was the best thing that could have happened to the place. He'd been raised on a ranch, himself, and had thought he would be taking over the family spread. However, his family had been forced to sell it before Tom had finished college.

There had been a time when Dan had thought Tom might end up being a part of the family. Tom's interest in Mandy had been obvious to Dan for some time, but once Rafe suddenly appeared in their lives again, Mandy's love for Rafe had made her blind to anyone else.

Dan stopped at the gate of the fence that surrounded the ranch house and the various barns and buildings, keeping the animals away from them. He got out and opened the gate, drove through, got out and closed the gate, then continued up the driveway to the main house.

As soon as he pulled up in front of the low stone fence that marked the beginning of the lawn encircling the house, Dan saw Tom walk to the wide door of the barn and look out to see who had arrived. With a sudden grin of recognition that shone blazing white in his tanned face, Tom loped over to the car.

"Well, look who's here!" he said, pounding Dan on the back. "Glad to see you back home, boss."

Dan stretched and rubbed his lower back while he looked around the place. "How have things been around here?"

"Can't complain. How about you? I almost didn't recognize you with that dark tan. Your vacation obviously agreed with you."

Dan reached behind the seat and pulled out his bag. "It must have. I woke up this morning too restless to sit around on the beach for another day. Figured it was time to head back home."

"Rafe will be glad to see your ugly mug," Tom said, with a lopsided grin.

"You think?"

"Oh, yeah. He's been busy trying to keep up with the company as well as preventing Mandy from charging off down there to check on you."

Dan shook his head. "You'd think having Kelly and Angie to look after would be enough for her these days."

"Actually, they've had four new arrivals in the past ten days that have kept Mandy and Maria running from daylight to past dark."

"Thank God Rafe's mom volunteered to help with our foster parenting program. How old are the kids?"

"Let's see, one's about Kelly's age—fourteen—two are brothers, eight and ten, and the little girl is six."

Dan laughed. "And they're going to teach the six-year-old how to help run the ranch? That I've got to see."

Tom nodded with a smile. "Well, she's been helping to feed the baby lambs, which instantly won her over."

Dan picked up his bag and said, "I've got some calls to make, so I'd better get going. Let's get together in the morning and go over any questions that might have come up in the past few weeks."

"Sounds good to me. It's good to have you back."

Dan let himself in the back door that led into the kitchen. The house was spotless. He had a hunch that was more of Mandy's work. He went back to his bedroom, tossed his bag on his bed and took a quick shower before dressing in jeans and a chambray shirt.

He called the office and asked to speak to Rafe.

Dan heard the click of the phone and Rafe say, "So how's the surf?"

"It was still a little rough when I left there this morning, but I think the storm has mostly blown itself out."

"Where are you now?"

"At the ranch."

There was a pause. "You're home?"

"Yep. Tom tells me we've had some new arrivals. How are they doing?"

Rafe groaned. "Oh, they're fine. I don't know if *we're* going to be able to keep up with them. I've never seen so much energy!"

"Mandy must be pleased."

"You haven't spoken to her?"

"Not yet. Thought I'd show up in time for dinner, looking pitiful, and maybe she and Maria will feel sorry for me and feed me.''

"Glad you're back.''

"Me, too. Uh, say, there was mention about applicants showing up at the office. Are you in a place where you could look up a name and phone number off of one of them for me?''

"Hold on.'' Dan heard another click, then was given an earful of upbeat music that made him grin. He wondered whose idea it was to entertain potential clients with recordings of some of Austin's finest musicians. If he wasn't mistaken, that was a Stevie Ray Vaughn number. Rafe came back on the line. "Who are you looking for?''

"Shannon Doyle.''

Sounding surprised, Rafe said, "How did you know that Shannon had been in?''

"I happened to run into her while I was on the island. I wanted to talk to her more about her job history, but she left before I got the chance.''

"She definitely looks qualified for almost anything you'd want her to do.''

"That doesn't surprise me. Where's she living?''

Rafe recited an apartment address in southwest Austin and gave him the phone number.

"Thanks. Are you coming home soon?'' Dan asked.

"You bet. I wouldn't want to miss the chewing out your loving sister has been preparing to give you.''

"Oh. Well, thanks for all your sympathy.''

Rafe laughed. "Don't mention it. I'll see you shortly.''

Dan hung up and stared at the phone number he had in front of him. He didn't know why he was so nervous about contacting her. They'd only spent a couple of days together and yet she had made an indelible impression on him.

He'd spent the past two days missing her. Now when he was only minutes away from hearing her voice again, he was getting cold feet.

He reminded himself that he was no longer a teenager. He was a grown man who had discovered something important about his life.

It was empty without Shannon Doyle's presence.

He picked up the phone and punched in the numbers.

# Twelve

The phone rang several times before Shannon answered, sounding breathless.

"H'lo?"

"Did I catch you at a bad time?"

There was a long pause before she replied. "Dan?"

He smiled, pleased that she recognized his voice. "That's right."

"How did you get this number?"

"You put it on your job application. Am I interrupting anything?"

"I was getting out of the shower when I heard the phone."

Dan had a sudden vision of Shannon standing there wearing little more than a towel while talking to him. He immediately grew rigid, dismayed and embarrassed by his instant reaction to the mere sound of her voice.

"I, uh, was wondering if you'd like to meet me at the office tomorrow. I want to talk to you."

"Where are you?"

"At the ranch."

"When did you get back?"

"Oh, about a half hour ago."

"You're going to work tomorrow?"

"I would say it's past time, wouldn't you?"

"I, uh, don't think it would be a good idea for me to work for you."

"That may be true. So why don't we discuss it in the morning…say around ten o'clock?" He waited, afraid she would refuse.

Finally, she said, "All right, ten o'clock."

"See you then," he said, and hung up.

Dan knew that he needed a plan. He could understand Shannon's embarrassment regarding her brother's actions. Somehow, someway, Dan intended to use Buddy's accusations to his benefit.

He wanted her. He was attracted to her like he'd never been to another woman, including his erstwhile fiancée. Therefore, he needed to get to know her better and to convince her that they could make a relationship work.

At least Buddy was on his side.

And the mysterious grandmother.

So he'd work on the plan, and meanwhile, would go face his sister.

"I can't believe it," Mandy said when he walked into the home she and Rafe had built on the ranch. "You decided to rejoin the human race."

Mandy was three years younger than he and Rafe, but she didn't look her age. She particularly didn't look old enough to be the mother of her adopted son, Kelly, who now towered over her and was watching the brother-sister reunion with a big grin on his face.

"Actually, it's called a vacation. I understand that people all over the world indulge in them with alarming regularity."

She chuckled and threw her arms around his neck. "I'm glad you're home."

He hugged her back. "So am I. If nothing else, maybe it will stop those blasted phone calls of yours."

"You would have been devastated if no one had noticed you'd disappeared, and you know it," she replied, laughing.

"How was the beach?" Kelly asked, as he sauntered to the large kitchen table and sprawled into one of the chairs. "Did you spot any serious bikini-bait down there?"

"Kelly," Mandy warned. "Watch your mouth."

He looked at her innocently. "What did I say?"

"Can't say that I noticed," Dan replied, sitting down as well.

Mandy rolled her eyes. "You're in worse shape than I thought."

Dan winked at Kelly. "You know, Mandy, I just got home a while ago. Haven't had a chance to get to the store for groceries. So I was wondering—" He left the question dangling.

She shook her head in amused exasperation. "I should have known you had an ulterior motive for showing up on my doorstep first thing. As it happens, Maria is cooking over at the Wranglers' Roost tonight and we're all invited."

"I understand you have new occupants."

She nodded, her eyes shining. "That's right. Three

counselors and four children. They seem to be settling in quite well.''

"I'm really pleased.''

Mandy sat down at the table with them. "It's a dream come true, Dan. We've been talking about this for so many years.''

"Maria's settled in okay at the Wrangler's Roost?''

"Yep. She took the rooms off the kitchen and made them her own. Rafe and I tried to talk her into staying here with us—we've certainly got enough room—but she insisted on having her own place. I'm just happy she wants to stay on the ranch after all these years of being out of touch with Rafe.''

They were still seated at the table when Rafe came through the door. His dark eyes took in his wife's sparkling mood, his son's amusement and his best friend's serenity in one quick glance.

"Look who finally wandered home,'' Mandy said, tilting her face for Rafe's kiss. He took his time, leaving her flushed and a little breathless before straightening. "How about a beer?'' he asked Dan, going to the refrigerator.

"Sounds good.''

"Where's Angie?'' he asked.

"Believe it or not, she's actually taking a nap. It took forever to get her down. At this rate,'' she said, glancing at the kitchen clock, "she'll be going strong half the night.''

"Did you reach Shannon?'' Rafe said, nudging the refrigerator door closed with his hip and handing Dan one of the bottles in his hand. Dan could have kicked him for bringing Shannon into the conversation. He wasn't ready to discuss her with Mandy just yet.

"Shannon?'' Mandy said, her head whipping around. "Are you talking about Shannon Doyle?''

Dan studied his sister's avid expression and said, "I wasn't aware you knew her," trying to side step the question.

She frowned at him. "Of course I know her. We went to school together. Don't you remember her?"

"Nope. Just her brother." He unconsciously rubbed his jaw. He had a hunch he'd remember Buddy for a very long time.

"Oh." Mandy started to say something, then fell silent.

Rafe lifted his brows, waiting for Dan to answer his question.

"Yeah. She's coming in for an interview at ten in the morning."

"We received several applications that look to be solid prospects."

"Good," Dan replied, taking a drink from the longneck bottle. "We may be filling more than one position. I've been giving the matter some thought. I'm not interested in working the long hours I was pulling down before. I may see about delegating more of the responsibility than I'd first thought when I decided to actively seek out prospects for employment."

"That makes sense," Rafe said.

Mandy once again started to say something, then seemed to think better of it. Her reticence amused Dan. She probably didn't want him yelling at her for attempting to direct his life.

Mandy pushed back from the table and said, "I'm going over to help Maria with supper. Will one of you listen for Angie?"

Kelly chuckled. "Oh, I don't think any of us could miss hearing her. She definitely lets everyone know when she's awake."

Once Mandy left, Dan said, "I had quite an experience while I was on the island."

"Yeah?" Rafe responded.

"Yep. I managed to get myself kidnapped."

Rafe had just taken a swallow of beer when Dan spoke. His chair had been resting on the back two legs. Now the chair fell forward and Rafe choked, spraying beer.

Kelly's response was a little more restrained. He straightened from his slouched position, his eyes twice their normal size.

Dan leaned over and pounded Rafe's back. "Sorry," he managed to say with a straight face.

"What the hell happened?" Rafe demanded.

"I saw these three men talking to Shannon. One of them grabbed her arm and I went over to even the odds a little. One of them knocked me out and took the two of us out to a yacht in the Gulf."

"You've got to be joking." Rafe stared at him in complete disgust.

"Hey, I know you could have handled those odds with no problem, hotshot, but you gotta remember that I haven't had your commando-style military training."

"Who the hell did this?"

"He introduced himself as Gianni Guardino. I'm assuming he's from St. Louis. He was quite polite, given the circumstances. It seems he was actually looking for information on Shannon's ex-boyfriend. He'd traced her to the island, and when she insisted to his men that she didn't know anything, they decided to let their boss question her. Because I jumped in trying to be heroic, I got to go along for the ride."

"My God, Dan. I can't turn my back on you for a moment without you getting involved in something dangerous.'' Rafe eyed him for several minutes. ''Wait a minute. Was that during this latest storm?''

''Oh yes.''

''How did you get back to land?''

''He dropped us off in Galveston. He was very affable and apologetic for inconveniencing us. Since we'd been taken on the beach and had no money with us, he kindly gave me a few hundred dollars to help us get home.''

Rafe shook his head. ''Only you, Dan, could possibly get into so much trouble without half trying.''

Dan laughed. ''I can't deny that, I'm afraid.'' He glanced over at Kelly. ''So why don't we just keep this to ourselves, all right? No sense in getting Mandy upset.''

Rafe was quick to agree.

Dan wasn't too sure he wanted to discuss anything else that happened, especially where Shannon was concerned, so he was relieved to hear noises from the other room which informed the males that fifteen-month-old Angie was ready for her adoring family to pay her some attention.

Dan had been at the office for several hours when Donna, the receptionist, buzzed him and informed him that Shannon had arrived.

''Show her in.''

He stood and walked to the door. He had just opened it when they appeared from down the hall. He held out his hand, ignoring his racing pulse at the sight of her dressed in a suit and high heels. ''It was good of you to meet with me, Shannon,'' he said pleasantly and nodded a dismissal to Donna. ''Won't you please come in?''

He had worn a sports jacket to work, but had long ago removed it, along with his tie. Unless he was meeting clients, Dan preferred to dress more casually and as Shannon had seen him in nothing more than a swimsuit, he saw no reason to dress more formally.

She, on the other hand, looked very professional and very distant.

And she'd yet to speak to him.

He waited for her to be seated, then walked around behind the desk and sat down. "Would you like some coffee?" he asked pleasantly.

"No, thank you," she replied in her husky voice.

He'd missed hearing her voice. He'd missed looking at her, talking to her, kissing her.

Dan faced the fact that he was in deep trouble.

He shuffled some of the papers on his desk and reminded himself that he could handle this meeting. Her papers were on top. He picked up her application and its attachment. "I'm impressed with your resume," he finally said.

"Dan, I—"

He waited, but when she said nothing more, he prompted her. "Yes?"

"I don't think this is a good idea."

"Yes, you did mention yesterday that you had some reservations about working with me."

"It would be a disaster."

"I see." He studied her for a long moment. "Well, if that's the way you feel, I'm not going to coerce you into considering what we have to offer here."

He stood and walked around the desk.

She, too, came to her feet, looking a little startled at the suddenness in which the interview ended.

"So if that's all of the interview, then I suggest we go shopping." He glanced at his watch. "We have a couple of hours before lunch. That should give us plenty of time to find—"

"Shopping?" she repeated weakly as though she'd never before heard the word.

He took her left hand and held it up between them. "For rings. I figure that's the first step in this getting married business."

"What are you talking about?"

He escorted her out of his office and to the back door of the building. His car was parked right outside. He opened the passenger door and stepped back, mentally keeping his fingers crossed that she'd go along with the idea. She first stared at him...then looked at the car...back to him...back to the car, then shook her head as though completely confused...and got inside. He closed the door very carefully and walked around the car.

As soon as he was seated, she spoke. "We aren't getting married, Dan," she said with a slight quiver in her voice. He leaned over and kissed her lightly on the lips, unable to go another moment without touching her.

"I gave my word," he replied solemnly before buckling his seat belt, checking to make sure hers was also fastened, and drove out of the DSC parking lot.

"Dan, this is ridiculous. I had a long talk with Buddy last night and explained to him that—"

"Your grandmother expects us to get married."

She massaged her forehead. "My grandmother—" she began, then stopped. "You don't know my grandmother," she explained nervously.

"I'm looking forward to meeting her as well as the rest of your family. You haven't mentioned your parents. Are they still alive?"

"My mother is. She and my grandmother still live on the ranch. My oldest brother Alan runs the place."

"What does Buddy do?"

"He's one of the football coaches at UT."

"Are you staying with him?"

She glanced at him in surprise. "No. Why would you think that?"

"I saw the Austin address."

She sighed. "I got my own apartment in town because I felt it would be easier to look for work from here."

"I was thinking of a Thanksgiving wedding myself," he said as though continuing a conversation.

"Thanksgiving! That's only two weeks away! What is the matter with you?"

He paused for a red light. "I know. It will be tough finding a church in that short a time, so my idea is this: why don't you ask your pastor if he would perform the ceremony at my ranch the Saturday after Thanksgiving? We'll get on the phone and call family and friends and informally invite them. If you want, we can make it a casual affair, although I would love to see you in a white wedding dress." The light turned green.

"Why are you doing this? To humiliate me? It wasn't bad enough that my brother turned into a Neanderthal? You have to go along with him?"

"I hardly think that marriage to me is going to cause you any humiliation, but I suppose it's all in the way you choose to look at things. I figure that two weeks is the absolute maximum time that I'll be able to keep from dragging you off to my bed and making mad, passionate love to you. You've stayed a virgin this long. I figure another two weeks won't kill me. But let's don't push our luck, okay?" He pulled into a shopping mall and cruised for a parking space before saying, "I figure as long as we don't find ourselves alone in a room with a bed, I'll be able to conduct myself in a manner befitting a gentleman."

He whipped into a space, hopped out and opened her door with a flourish.

Shannon slowly unfastened her seat belt, reluctantly took his proffered hand and stepped out of the car. "I think you need to see a doctor about the blow to your head, Dan. You're delusional."

He smiled and tucked her hand inside his. "I brought my mother's ring along to have it sized, but I also wanted to pick out matching bands for us and I know just where I want to get them."

A well-known local artist made exquisite jewelry. He wanted something special—nothing gaudy—and nothing overpowering. After all, Shannon was a small person, with delicate hands. He couldn't have her wearing something that would weigh her down.

They entered the mall and walked into Everly Jewelers.

"Dan, we can't do this," she said in an undertone, glancing at the customers already there. "I don't know what Buddy said to you, but I assure you that this is no way to make a relationship work."

He smiled. "Well, we have two weeks to find out how compatible we are. Personally, I think we have a great many things in common. I was looking forward to having you take part in the business, but if you—"

"You expect me to marry you as well as work with you?"

"Sounds like the perfect solution to me. By the time we leave the office we'll be ready to think of something else to do with ourselves. We won't have to waste time catching each other up on our day."

She rubbed her forehead as though she might be getting a headache. "I'd like to think that I'm dreaming…that I'll wake up any time now." She looked around her, closed her eyes, and then reopened them.

"Don't you want to marry me, Shannon?" he asked, taking both her hands in his and looking into her beautiful eyes. He felt that he could drown in them and die happy.

"That's not the point," she replied, cheering him immeasurably. She hadn't said that she didn't want to marry him. He was making progress.

"The point is," he explained quietly, "that I have agreed to marry you. I don't know why you have a problem with it. I don't."

"This is serious."

"I know. That's why we're here in a jewelry store, ready to choose wedding bands."

"I mean, we can't just decide to get married. We don't know each other."

"I certainly intend to remedy that as soon as possible." He turned and walked over to the display case. "Now then, let's see how our taste in jewelry meshes."

# Thirteen

Shannon woke up the morning of Thanksgiving—just two days before her scheduled wedding—certain that she had lost touch with reality, not to mention her common sense.

The first thing she saw hanging on the door to her closet was her wedding dress, proof positive that she had misplaced her ability to make rational decisions. She glanced down at her hand, at the ring that had once belonged to Dan's mother. Her engagement ring.

Ever since the day she'd stood there in the jewelry store and watched him pay an unholy amount of money for matching wedding bands, she'd been in some kind of time warp, allowing things to flow around her without once stopping the world to explain that of course she wasn't going to marry Dan Crenshaw.

The whole idea was absurd.

The problem was that she was fighting her own feelings

as well as Dan's assault on her senses. Choosing their rings for a nonexistent wedding had been just the first step in his insistent plan to make her aware of him.

As if there was a remote possibility that she could remove him from her mind.

He somehow managed to see her every day despite his busy schedule. Not only that, but when he was around her, he always seemed to be touching her in some way— his hand would casually rest at her waist, or he would lightly caress her shoulder or hold her hand. In addition, he continued to kiss her at the least provocation.

How could he do this to her? She'd been thrown back into those horrible adolescent years of yearning for him— those years when she had daydreamed about being noticed by Dan Crenshaw. What was she expected to do now that he had finally noticed her—with a vengeance?

Well, for one thing, she'd managed to get over her childhood crush on him. She no longer idolized him. She'd been given plenty of chances to see his feet of clay.

Nope, the crush was gone forever.

Instead, she'd fallen deeply and irrevocably in love with him.

Which was why there was a wedding dress hanging on the door taunting her. Well, that and the fact that her grandmother had insisted on the shopping expedition. Buddy must have convinced her grandmother that what he'd found going on at the island definitely called for an early wedding.

None of Shannon's explanations or protestations seemed to make a difference to her grandmother.

On more than one occasion Shannon had attempted to discuss the matter with her mother, but to no avail. Her mother merely shrugged and reminded her that grandmother had a very strong will. Shannon's mother loved and honored Shannon's grandmother and seldom attempted to cross her.

Her mother assured Shannon that she wasn't about to cross her over the necessity for Shannon to marry a man with whom she had shared an apartment and possibly a bed.

In little more than an hour Dan would arrive to escort Shannon to the ranch where he was throwing a party for friends and family to celebrate Thanksgiving. There would be plenty of smoked turkeys as well as barbecued ribs and brisket.

It would be the first time both sides of the family had gotten together, although Shannon had spoken to Mandy by phone on several occasions since she'd returned from the island. Each time she had hoped to gain her assistance in convincing Dan that what he intended to do was not a good idea.

Mandy merely laughed and called it bridal jitters.

Shannon was not looking forward to the gathering of the clans today.

Nevertheless, she was ready when Dan knocked on her door. She opened it and, as usual when coming face to face with him after an absence, fought the urge to throw herself around his neck and kiss him senseless.

It just wasn't fair that one man should have such a strong effect on her.

"Mornin', sunshine," he drawled, stepping into the room. He gathered her in his arms and took his time giving her a very thorough kiss. When he finally raised his head, his smile was strained. "Enough of that, now. We've got to get out of here. Just hold that thought for two more days, okay?"

His kisses weakened her to the point that she wasn't certain she could stand, much less hold a thought.

''Did I tell you that you're looking particularly fetching this mornin'?'' he asked, once he'd backed away to arm's length.

Seeing him in his snug, faded jeans and soft, knit shirt—which emphasized his broad shoulders, sculptured chest and muscular arms—made Shannon want to whimper and gnaw on her knuckles.

''You ready to go?'' he asked, cocking his head. ''You haven't said a word since I walked in here.''

She took a couple of deep breaths and smiled. ''Good morning, Dan.''

He grinned and kissed her again, for good measure.

''We're going to have fun today,'' he said, taking her hand and leading her out the door. ''This is our rehearsal dinner, you know. I figure everybody's going to be here that will come on Saturday. You did say your pastor was willing to come to the ranch, didn't you?''

She nodded. ''I believe that Grandmother convinced him it was the thing to do.''

They went down the stairs to the parking lot and Dan helped her into his car. ''I'm looking forward to meeting your grandmother. She must be quite a woman.''

''Oh, yes, she certainly is.''

''Buddy's coming today, isn't he?''

''Yes, although he's not part of the wedding party. Alan will be giving me away.''

''Maybe we should have Buddy as ring bearer. After all, he's instrumental in making this marriage a reality.''

''Oh, I'm very well aware of that. But he couldn't have done it without you caving in so quickly.''

Dan laughed. ''Well, he has a mean uppercut, I'm telling you. The thought of doing anything that might cause Buddy to become riled will keep me on the straight and narrow path for years to come.''

She didn't smile. "I know better. You aren't afraid of him. I've been trying to figure out for the past two weeks why you're insisting on marrying me."

"What have you decided?"

"Someone is blackmailing you into doing it."

"Bingo. You got it, first guess." He stopped at a light. "I'm sorry to be rushing you this morning, but I left my foreman in charge of the smoker and we need to get back to get everything set up for all the company."

"So who's blackmailing you?" she asked once they were on their way out of Austin.

"Beats me. Why can't you just accept the fact that I'm willing to marry you and let it go at that?"

She stared out the window for several miles without speaking. She couldn't tell him how much it ate at her that his motives for this marriage were so unclear. If he loved her, he would have said so. If he didn't love her, why go through this charade? And what if, after they were married, he met someone and fell in love? How would Shannon be able to deal with the possible heartbreak that would cause her?

"I suppose it's because I don't think you're taking any of this seriously. You're treating marriage as though it were some game."

"I believe in marriage, which is why I'm still unmarried at thirty-three," he replied. "I didn't want to make a mistake. When I marry, it will be for keeps."

"Then if you're planning to make a lifetime commitment, don't you think you need to put more time and thought into it?"

"I have."

"Two weeks?"

"Let me put it this way. I've got a good business sense about me. I know how to weigh options, judge people and make rapid decisions. I don't know why you chose to come down to the island and move in with me. I no longer care. But I don't think you would have done that if you hadn't trusted me and believed that I wouldn't take advantage of you. Would you agree with that assessment?"

"I suppose."

He grinned. "Marriage is an honorable solution. Besides that, and this you already know, I'm having a tough time keeping my hands off of you."

She looked down pointedly at his hand presently resting on her thigh.

He laughed. "Believe me, this is me on my best behavior. Because I consider myself a gentleman, I am not going to seduce you, at least not until my wedding ring is on your finger."

"So the truth is, you're in lust with me."

He grinned. "Close enough. Have I told you what I have planned for our honeymoon?"

She rolled her eyes. "No."

"A friend is going to fly us down to the island in his plane. We'll stay at the condo for a few days and he'll come back to get us."

"You make it sound so simple."

"It is, actually. I have the landing strip at the ranch. I've used his services to get me around the country for several years. We'll spend our time alone instead of traveling. Besides, I'm still hoping to coax you into working for the company. I've got lots of catching up to do between now and Christmas. My plan is to convince you to help me."

Now she had another concern. Was he marrying her for her business skills?

She was going to drive herself crazy trying to figure out Dan Crenshaw.

"This is the first time I've been to your ranch," she said several miles later.

"I know. I apologize. Things have been a little hectic since I got back from the island. But the family is looking forward to seeing you after all this time. You saw Rafe when you came in to interview. Mandy says she can't remember the last time she saw you and is eager for you to get to know Angie, my niece."

Good ol' Mandy. Shannon couldn't very well let on that they had been in close communication without letting Dan and Rafe know Mandy's part in Shannon's visit to the island.

Not that Shannon minded keeping the secret. She saw no reason for Dan to get upset with Mandy for explaining to Shannon what was going on in his life. There were times when what you don't know can't upset you.

Dan pulled through the gate to the ranch, gave Shannon a quick smile and silently prayed that he could pull today off. He didn't mind admitting to himself that he was nervous. He wanted the world to think that he was absolutely, positively comfortable with the idea of getting married.

When the truth was he was scared to death.

What did he know about marriage? They didn't teach husband skills in school. So much had changed in the world since his folks had married. Their life together was the only example he had. Somehow he couldn't see Shannon going along with his dad's way of doing things.

And yet, here he was. Moving heaven and earth in order to marry Shannon Doyle.

She had bewitched him. He wasn't sure how or when. All he knew was that he couldn't let this woman walk out of his life.

Now he was taking her to meet his family for the first

time. At the same time he would be meeting her family. He'd been preparing himself for her grandmother. He figured Buddy must have gotten his physique from her, the way everyone seemed so afraid of her.

Well, she couldn't be mad at him, now, could she? He'd agreed to marriage, just the way she'd wanted it. In fact, Dan was grateful to her—he could count on her to make sure that Shannon didn't back out at the last minute.

When he pulled up in front of the house, he was relieved to note that Rafe and Mandy hadn't arrived with their group. He glanced at his watch. They should have almost an hour before their company started to arrive.

"Dan, your place is beautiful."

He was relieved to hear the admiration in her voice. "Thanks. It's typical ranch-style living." He helped her out of the car. "There's nothing fancy about the place."

"I like it."

He led her up the steps to the porch and opened the back door. Few people ever used the front door. "I'll show you around the house, then we'll go check with Tom to see how everything's progressing."

He followed Shannon as she wandered through the kitchen and dining room, then crossed the hallway to the living room and den. The house had been built almost fifty years before. It had been remodeled several times, with extra rooms added. He'd updated the kitchen a few years ago.

When they got to the master bedroom, he paused in the doorway and watched as she looked around the large room. "Of course, you know that you can make any changes you want," he said quietly. "Whatever you don't like, just get rid of it."

She peeked into the bathroom, then glanced over her shoulder. "Did you design this, by chance?"

He settled against the doorjamb, staying across the room from her. She looked so damn sexy in her slim jeans and silk blouse, he knew better than to venture any closer.

"Yeah, I did. I wanted a place to relax."

"That tub's big enough for a small party."

He grinned. "Maybe we'll have one of our own in a week or so."

He watched her turn a rosy-pink and hastily leave the bathroom. "Maybe we should check with your foreman now."

"Good idea." He deliberately waited until she reached his side, then wrapped his arm around her shoulders and they walked back down the hall.

When he opened the back door and stepped out on the porch, Dan saw that two vans had pulled up. He grinned at the logo on the side of the newer, white van—Wranglers' Roost, encircled by a lariat.

Mandy had chosen the name for the part of the ranch that had been designated for the foster children who had finally found a home. He watched them as they scrambled out of the van and charged around the house to the area where the smoke sent out aromatic signals of good things to come.

In the other van, Mandy, Kelly, Maria, and Rafe, carrying Angie, got out. Dan felt Shannon tense beside him. "C'mon, now. You remember Rafe and Mandy. Now you're going to meet Rafe's mom, son and daughter."

Mandy was the first to speak. "Shannon, it's so good to finally see you after all this time." She threw her arms around her and hugged her. "I've been fussing at Dan for not bringing you out here sooner. Instead, here he waits until two days before the wedding." She looked over at Dan and added, "He was probably afraid we'd tell you all we know about him and you'd run for the hills." She turned and gave Dan a hug. "You're looking mighty proud of yourself these days, big brother."

Rafe stood a few feet away with Angie in his arms. She was chattering and waving her hands. "Let her get a word in edgewise, Mandy," he admonished, nodding his head to Shannon. "Good to see you," he said.

Now that she was surrounded by Dan's family, Shannon felt for the first time as though all of this was real—the engagement, the ring, the dress, and their plans to be married in two days. She hadn't expected the size of the ranch, the large, comfortable home, or the way she felt part of the family.

Dan introduced her to Mrs. McClain, Rafe's mom, and to Kelly, who blushed and suddenly got very interested in the dog dancing around his feet. She played peek-a-boo with Angie over Rafe's shoulder. She happened to glance up and catch Dan watching her intently. She wondered what he was thinking. His eyes seemed to probe deep inside of her, searching out all of her secrets.

He claimed her hand and said, "Let's go check on Tom. I don't know about the rest of you, but I'm starving."

The group of them followed Dan to a paved pavilion where the smoker was located. Picnic tables were set up, ready for food.

Mandy said, "Guess I'd better unload the food from the van. Shannon, care to join me?"

Grateful for a respite from Dan's dynamic presence, she nodded and returned to the driveway with Mandy.

"Who would have guessed this would be the way things worked out?" Mandy said as soon as they were out of earshot of the men.

"Dan's lost his mind," Shannon muttered.

Mandy grinned. "Oh, I don't think so. He just needed

a wake-up call and you were just the person to deliver it. I can't remember when I've seen him look so relaxed and happy, and yet, according to Rafe, he's been putting in tremendously long hours since he returned. But he has a new attitude that is wonderful to see. You're a miracle worker, Shannon.''

"But to be *marrying* him!''

"You love him, don't you?''

Mandy certainly believed in going right to the point. Shannon saw no reason to lie. "Yes. Very much.''

"And he's besotted with you. It's hard not to laugh when I see him being so possessive of you. When he and Sharon were together, he ignored her most of the time. It's no wonder she decided to back out.''

"He doesn't talk about her.''

"There's nothing to tell. I think he decided it was time to get married, picked someone he thought would make him a good wife, and proceeded with his plans. I don't think he gave a thought to his own feelings.''

"But Mandy, this is such a vulnerable time for him.''

Mandy paused in placing covered dishes on large trays and handing them to Shannon. "Yes, it is. He finally dropped all his shields and other defenses and allowed himself to feel. It's a beautiful sight to behold.'' She picked up the other tray and started toward the house. "Let's get these inside and find utensils. When do you expect your family to get here?''

Shannon sighed. "I don't know. Alan and his wife are supposed to go to her folks' place, then drop by here later. Buddy said he'd make sure that Mom and Grandmother had a ride.''

Once inside the kitchen, the women placed the trays on the table and countertops. Mandy took Shannon's hand and squeezed it. "Everything's going to be fine. Just think. We'll be doing this again in two days. Won't we have fun?''

Shannon felt overwhelmed. She had a hunch this was just the beginning.

# Fourteen

When the women came outside carrying the food, they found the children chasing each other around the yard with a couple of dogs leaping and barking, wanting to get in on the fun. There was noise and laughter all around.

Shannon loved it. As soon as she appeared Dan took her over to a tall, good-looking man with blond hair and clear, silver-gray eyes.

"Shannon, this is Tom Parker, my foreman. Tom, this is Shannon. I saw her first."

Tom grinned and took her hand in his. "It's a real pleasure to meet you, ma'am. I can certainly understand Dan's rush to get you in front of a preacher."

"You can let go of her hand, now, Tom," Dan said, causing everyone to laugh.

"Looks like the meat's ready," Rafe said, peering inside the large round barbecue smoker. "You think we can get those kids to sit still long enough to eat?"

Mandy chuckled. "It's a wonder they haven't already attacked the food. This is the first time any of them have attended a barbecue. That's all they've been talking about for the past several days."

"Well," Dan replied, "we could go ahead and have them start filling their plates. Shannon's folks should be getting here any time now."

As though that was the cue, they heard a truck pull up. Everyone turned to look.

It was Buddy.

He was alone.

Shannon hurried over to him. He was climbing out of the truck when she asked in a panic, "Where's Mom and Grandmother?"

"Hold on, sis, nothing's wrong. Grandmother said she was feeling a little tired this morning. She said she wanted to be sure she felt up to par by Saturday, so she decided to spend the day resting. Of course Mom stayed home with her. She sent her best regards to everyone"

"Are you sure Grandmother is all right?"

He dropped his arm around her and gave her a reassuring hug. "Yeah, I think so. Maybe the excitement of the wedding has been a little much for her. I told her you'd understand why she couldn't make it. She promised she would be here Saturday."

Dan joined them as they drew closer to the pavilion. "Is something wrong?"

"Not really," Shannon said. "My grandmother and mom decided not to come. Grandmother promises to be here Saturday, though."

She stepped away from Buddy and Dan enfolded her in his arms. "I'm sorry, sweetheart. I know you're disappointed."

She realized that she was. Very much. She'd been eager

for her grandmother to meet Dan. Now she wouldn't meet him until their wedding day. It couldn't be helped.

She looked over at Buddy. "Are Alan and Sue still coming?"

"Yeah, but it won't be until around four. They said to save them some ribs. They expect to be all turkeyed out."

By the time her oldest brother and his wife arrived, Shannon finally had relaxed and begun to enjoy the activities. Dan greeted them as soon as they got there, making them feel welcomed.

She'd watched him all day as he got acquainted with the children, playing touch football with the older ones along with Rafe, having a serious discussion with Tami, the six-year-old, about her new doll and the tea party they would have with her new dishes.

How could she not love the man? She found him distractingly handsome, but beyond that, he was a good man. An honorable man.

And he was going to be her husband in two days.

If this was all a dream, then please, God, she prayed, don't let her wake up.

It was late evening before everyone packed up and went home, leaving Dan and Shannon alone for the first time in several hours.

"I hate to have you drive all the way into Austin to take me home," Shannon said.

Dan glanced at his watch. It was almost ten o'clock. The time had gone by amazingly fast, considering the fact he hadn't been able to spend much time with Shannon.

It also bothered him that he hadn't met her mother and grandmother. He wondered if he should suggest going to see them tomorrow. But for the moment, he just wanted to settle back and spend a little time with his intended.

"You could always stay here," he suggested, holding the screen door open and letting her walk past him into the kitchen. The hall light was on, which gave off some illumination, but the room was shadowy. He pushed the door closed behind him.

She turned and looked at him. "Oh, that would really get everyone to talking."

He threw his arms out in an innocent gesture. "We've got three bedrooms here."

"You think Buddy will believe I slept in another room?"

He grinned. "What more can he do to me? I'm marrying you in about forty hours." His grin widened. "Not that I'm counting, or anything."

She walked over to him and slid her arms around his waist. "Well, cowboy, you've talked me into it," she said, going up on her toes and kissing him.

His heart charged into a fast gallop at her words. Rather than question his good fortune, he wrapped his arms around her and returned the kiss.

She felt so good in his arms, just where he wanted to keep her for the rest of his life. He picked her up and carried her into the living room without relinquishing her lips. He sank into his most comfortable easy chair, still cradling her in his arms.

"You're looking proud of yourself for some reason," she murmured, drawing back from him slightly.

"I'm not surprised. I have you right where I want you."

"What—exactly—do you intend to do about it?"

He decided to show her. With slow, deliberate movements he carefully unbuttoned her silk blouse and slid it off her shoulders. Then he reached behind her and unfastened her bra, gently pulling it away as well.

"I thought we might want to get a little better acquainted," he admitted before he smoothed his hand down from her neck to her shoulders, trailing his fingers until he cupped one of her breasts. He leaned over her and touched his tongue to its crest. She shivered, but made no effort to stop him.

"You taste as good as you look," he whispered, his tongue flicking across the pebbled surface. She shifted, and her breathing became a little uneven. Good. He wanted to affect her as strongly as she did him.

She slipped her hand beneath his shirt and caressed his chest. Chills chased over him. He refused to let her distract him now that he had her to himself, looking flushed and excited.

Before he was through, she would definitely know what it was like to have a man kiss and caress her. He cupped her other breast, kissing and stroking one, then the other, tugging on the nipples with his lips, causing her to gasp and catch her breath.

She finally lifted his head and blindly sought his mouth with hers. Her kiss fanned the flames that had been steadily building within him since she'd first opened her door to him that morning. He took over with mind-numbing kisses that seemed to go on and on, pausing only long enough for them to get some air before possessing her again.

By the time he finally raised his head, she lay in his arms—limp—her eyes closed. Her mouth was moist and slightly swollen, her lower lip too tempting to resist. He leaned down and nibbled, stroked, nibbled some more.

He couldn't keep his hand still as he cupped and caressed her breasts, stroking her from her throat to the top of her jeans, then molding his hand around her breasts, teasing the tips.

"Are you asleep?" he asked.

"Oh, yes. Just drifted off," she replied, teasing him, then reached up and tugged at his hair. "You know exactly what you're doing to me."

"Uh-huh."

"You know I won't be able to go to sleep now. I'll lie awake all night."

"Uh-huh."

"This is some kind of plot, isn't it?"

"Uh-huh."

She poked him in the shoulder with her fist.

"You Doyles are pretty quick with your fists, aren't you?" he asked, unable to hide his amusement.

She opened her eyes. "And don't you forget it. If you give me any trouble, I'll just call Buddy to come straighten you out."

"I'm scared."

"I can see that."

He leaned over and once again kissed her bared breast, tugged on the nipple, then quickly licked it. "I can't get over how tiny you are. Especially compared to Buddy."

"Buddy's built like my Uncle Raymond. He played pro-ball once upon a time."

Dan reluctantly sat her up in his lap and entwined his fingers with hers. "I promise you that you will not be sorry you were forced to marry me, Shannon."

"Nobody's forcing me, Dan."

"All right. But you haven't been given much room to change your mind."

"Is that what you're afraid will happen?"

He shrugged. "The thought did cross my mind a time or two."

She looked down at the solitaire on her left hand. "Giving me your mother's ring was a master stroke, Dan. It's almost as though everything you told Mr. Guardino has come to pass—the engagement, the ring."

"Your family's objections…"

"On the contrary, Buddy mentioned today that he hadn't even bothered looking for his old shotgun, he was that sure of your intentions."

"That's good to know. I can breathe easier now."

She took his face between her hands. "I just don't ever want you to regret this. We haven't known each other long enough to be getting married, you know. We're both taking a giant leap of faith, going into this blindly."

"I know. But I didn't want to take any chances that you'd hook up with another Rick Taylor. You've already pointed out to me your flawed judgment where men are concerned."

"Gee, thanks. What a timely reminder that is!"

"Speaking of time…I hate to end this beautiful evening, but I've got a full day of work facing me tomorrow. I need to get some sleep." He laughed. "Not that I'll be able to sleep much knowing you're just down the hallway."

"But we only have two more nights away from each other."

He hugged her to him. "Yes. After that, I never intend to go to bed without you right there in my arms."


By midafternoon of the next day, Dan was ready to pull his hair out. The supervisor had discovered that one of their orders had been filled wrong, two shipments were waiting to be picked up and the delivery service was running late. He had a stack of paperwork that had mushroomed—tripling its size from when he'd left the office the evening before Thanksgiving.

So when the receptionist buzzed him, Dan was not in the best of humor. "What is it, Donna?" he growled, trying to read a note from one of their suppliers that had come in on e-mail.

"Uh, sorry, Dan, but there's a lady here to see you. She said she doesn't have an appointment, but that she's sure you'll want to see her."

At the moment he couldn't think of anyone that he would particularly want to see unless she could help him to dig out from under all this paperwork.

"Did she give her name?"

"Kamiko Usura Stevens."

"Kamiko Stevens? I don't know anyone by that name. Did she say why she was here?"

"No, sir."

He sighed in disgust. Just what he needed. "All right. I'll come out there to see her."

He tossed down the phone and headed for the door. Who in the world could this be? And why would she be coming to see him today, of all days?

He strode down the hall and into the reception area. And stopped. There waiting for him was a diminutive woman no taller than four-feet, maybe ten inches or so, with silver hair and a benign expression, waiting for him, watching him out of large, black, almond-shaped eyes.

Shannon's eyes.

"Mrs. Stevens?" he asked, walking over to her. "I'm Dan Crenshaw. I'm so pleased that you have come to see me. Won't you come back to my office?"

"You know who I am?" she asked in a soft voice.

He smiled. "I believe that you may be Shannon's grandmother. Am I right?"

She nodded her head in a graceful and regal manner. "That is correct."

He turned to the receptionist. "Would you bring us some—" he looked at Kamiko, "would you like coffee or tea, perhaps?"

"Tea would be nice."

"Some tea, please," he said, offering his arm.

Kamiko took it and walked with him back to his office.

"I hope you'll excuse my messy office. It's just that—"

"Please," she said, holding up her hand. "It was rude of me to come without an invitation, but it was very important for me to speak with you today."

*Good grief, had she already discovered that Shannon had stayed at the ranch last night? If so, she must have her spies everywhere!*

He placed one of the visitor chairs closer to his desk and motioned for her to be seated. Then he returned to his chair and sat down.

"Actually, I'm very glad you decided to stop in," he said with a smile. "I have wanted to meet you. I was sorry to hear that you weren't feeling well enough to join us yesterday."

"Yes. That is the reason I'm here. I am suffering from a guilty conscience," she said quietly. Her hands were folded and rested in her lap. How many times had he seen Shannon sit that way—so still, so dignified.

He grinned. "You know, you're nothing like I expected you to be."

"Didn't Shannon tell you that I was born in Japan?"

"Actually, we haven't spent much time talking about family. I figure we have the rest of our lives for that."

"My daughter is quite put out with me, you know," she said in her soft voice. "She says I have been meddling too much and have caused problems for my granddaughter."

"You only wanted to protect her. I understand that."

She nodded, her face grave. "Yes. I want her to be protected. But I also want her to be loved. My daughter reminded me how I went against my upbringing and my family by marrying Sherman Stevens. I ignored everything I had been taught. Instead, I followed the promptings of my heart."

"How did the two of you meet?"

"It was a few months before the bombing at Pearl Harbor. He was in the Navy and stationed in Hawaii at the time. I was visiting relatives there. We met and fell in love. It was all very sudden. I was supposed to return home. Instead, we eloped and I stayed with him. It was very difficult for us after the bombing. I had become the enemy, you see."

"It must have been extremely hard for you to accept that your country was fighting your husband's country."

"Yes. His superior officers treated him with suspicion. The other wives, of course, left me to myself. But we got through that time."

There was a tap on the door and Donna entered, bringing a tray with tea. Dan wondered where she'd found the teapot, but didn't ask.

"Thank you," he said, taking the tray and setting it on the desk. Donna had also brought sugar, lemon and cream. Kamiko smiled at the display and poured the tea.

"What I have had to face these past two weeks," Kamiko went on to say, "is that I have forced my beloved granddaughter into a relationship not of her choosing."

Dan felt like a tight fist had suddenly squeezed his heart. "I don't think you've forced her, exactly," he replied.

"I am not unaware that younger generations look at love and marriage in a different way from when I was young. I have imposed my values on Shannon. Had she argued with me, she knew that I would have been deeply distressed. So she did not argue after she explained what happened."

He leaned forward. "She isn't unhappy about tomorrow, is she?" he asked urgently.

"It is I who am unhappy."

"I see. And what is it you would like me to do?"

"If Shannon wishes to marry, then I would like her husband to be one of her own choosing, just as I chose the man I wanted to marry. I have been forcing my will on her as my family attempted to do to me. I defied them and followed my heart. I would like my granddaughter to do the same."

"Then you never had any intention of making her marry me?"

She gave him a steady look. "Shannon has convinced me that you have never been intimate with her. I believe her."

"That is correct."

"If there was a chance that my granddaughter might be pregnant, I would not be here today."

"I see."

"Do you?"

"You have come to tell me that the wedding has been called off."

She nodded once again. "I cannot in good conscience sit by and allow this to happen. My daughter was right. I had planned to come to your Thanksgiving celebration yesterday and tell you both that I was wrong. But I couldn't face everyone. It was too much for me. I convinced myself that I had already meddled enough and that it would be better to allow events to continue without further interference on my part. This morning, I knew that I could not in good conscience remain silent.''

"Does Shannon know that you have come to see me?''

"Not yet. My daughter is waiting in the car for me. Once we leave here, we will go and speak with Shannon.''

"I see.''

"I hope you will forgive an old woman for involving herself so disruptively in your life.''

"There's nothing to forgive. If it will make you feel any better to know this, I wanted to marry Shannon for one simple reason—I love her.''

"But you don't know her, Mr. Crenshaw,'' she replied in a gentle voice.

"In all the ways that are important, Mrs. Stevens, I feel as though I know her very well. As you said, my heart spoke to me. It's only recently that I've bothered to listen to my heart. I've been amazed by what I've learned.''

She smiled. "That is a very good thing. Then if you truly love my granddaughter, you will give her the freedom of choice she deserves. She has been rushed into making this commitment, you see.''

"Yes, I do see that. I guess I've always known it.''

Kamiko stood. "Thank you for your kindness in hearing me out, Dan.''

He, too, stood and walked around the desk. "I wish that I had met you much earlier. Perhaps I could have convinced you that a marriage between Shannon and me would be a lasting one.''

"There is no hurry. Everything in its own time.''

Dan felt as though all the oxygen was being forced out of his lungs, as though he had to concentrate on every breath in order to have enough air to continue to speak.

"Thank you for explaining yourself to me,'' he said

and took her hand. He looked down at it, so small, so like
Shannon. He looked into her eyes, facing her scrutiny
without flinching.

He had nothing to hide.

He walked her back to the reception area. He even held
the door open for her, then watched as she walked to a
late-model automobile and got in. He saw the figure of
another woman behind the wheel and nodded, then returned to his office.

Of course she was right. He hadn't been fair to Shannon. Nor had her grandmother.

He idly wondered why doing the right thing hurt so
much?

# Fifteen

"**D**an?" Rafe called from the back door of the house. "Are you here? Where are you? What are you doing sitting in here in the dark?"

He paused in the archway between the hallway and the living room.

Dan sat in his recliner and stared at the blank screen of the television, a glass of Scotch in his hand. He turned his head. "What are you doing here?"

"Mandy thought we should be doing something to celebrate your last night as a single man. I told her we hadn't planned anything, but she thought you might want some company." He walked into the room and sat down, then reached over and turned on a lamp. "What the hell is going on?"

"Nothing much," Dan replied. He felt numb, which was a good feeling. He'd been sitting here ever since he'd gotten home from work, thinking about his life, about going to the island, about meeting Shannon. "I've been reminiscing, I suppose."

Rafe looked at his drink. "How many of those have you had?"

Dan glanced at his glass and smiled. "This is the first. Actually, I think it's mostly melted ice. I forgot to drink it." He met Rafe's serious gaze. "Relax, pal. I've already tried that route. It's a waste of good booze."

"I had no idea that you would mourn the end of your bachelorhood this way. I'm surprised."

"Actually, I'm feeling a little discouraged. I can't quite seem to get a bride all the way to the altar."

"What are you talking about?"

"Remember Sharon? No, of course not. You were overseas when I was engaged to her. Well, she was smart enough to back out before making the mistake of marrying me. You gotta admit I pick smart women. They're just too smart to marry me."

"Are you saying that Shannon has called off the wedding?"

"Well, metaphorically speaking, her grandmother decided to lower the shotgun that had been the motivating factor for us to get married."

"Her grandmother!"

"She carries a lot of weight in that family." He smiled. "Which is funny, when you think about it. She probably weighs all of ninety pounds soaking wet. I'm still having trouble adjusting to the idea that Buddy Doyle is any kin to her."

"I think I'll have a drink," Rafe said, getting up. "Because none of this is making any sense to me sober." He headed for the kitchen. "I hope you've got some beer in here."

"Oh, yeah. I'm fully stocked, ready for tomorrow's celebration.'' Dan looked at his watery drink and set it down. ''How about bringing me one?''

Rafe returned with two bottles. ''I'm not sure I should be doing this. You're not making sense sober. Who knows how garbled all of this will get if you start drinking.''

He settled back down and placed his booted feet on the coffee table. ''So tell me how come granny carries so much weight in the family.''

Dan heaved a sigh. ''Guess they all respect her. Whatever she says goes. That sort of thing. She told Buddy to find out what was going on between Shannon and me at the beach. He caught me half-asleep. I wasn't tracking well enough to figure out why he was there. He got a look at Shannon in her sexy little nightie and figured the two of us had been having our own good time and that I shouldn't be able to walk away without some kind of justice being enacted.''

''Were you?''

''Was I what?''

''Sleeping with her.''

''Nope. Not that I didn't want to, you understand. And technically, we did sleep together on that yacht, meaning we shared the same bed, and we both slept, at least until the storm kept us awake.''

Rafe started laughing.

''What's so damned funny?''

''You. This sudden decision to marry was a shotgun affair? Who are we kidding here? You're crazy about her.''

''Yeah. I know that. But what nobody has ever bothered to find out is how Shannon feels. Her grandmother was right. Shannon was going along with all of this out of respect for her grandmother. She didn't want to marry me. All she wanted was a chance to apply for a position at the company.'' He took a long drink from the bottle of beer. "Don't you find that funny, Rafe? She didn't want to marry me. She wanted to work for me. What happened to the days when a woman got a job in hopes of marrying her boss? Well, it sure as hell doesn't happen in *this* generation! A woman doesn't need a husband to make it in this world. She can be independent and lead her own life.''

"Uh-huh. Have you talked to Shannon about this?''

"No need. Her grandmother intended to confess her mistake and ask for forgiveness. Shannon's probably so relieved that she's out celebrating her newly found freedom tonight.''

"I had sincerely hoped that you'd worked through your 'poor me' phase. Guess you've hit another round of it.''

Dan looked at Rafe in surprise. "What the hell are you talking about?''

"Just listen to yourself. You've automatically jumped to the conclusion that, given a choice, no woman is going to want to marry you. Why should she? You're ugly as a mud fence, with no education, no street smarts, barely eking out an existence in a hand-to-mouth way. What could you possibly have to offer? Shannon's certainly had a close call, hasn't she?''

"You know, Rafe, there are times when you can be one mean son of a—'' he cleared his throat, ''—gun. Poor me, is it?''

"Sure sounds like it. I find you sitting in the dark, staring at nothing, gripping a drink in your hand. All the signs of a pity-party in full swing.''

"You think this is bad, you should have seen me on the island.''

"That was different.''

"Yeah? How's that?'' Dan asked.

"You'd been working your butt off for a company that was being sabotaged by your trusted partner. He almost got you nailed for it. When something that traumatic happens to any of us, we're forced to examine everything we believe in, including ourselves. It takes time to work through all the ways we view the world. We see ourselves differently. We have to figure out who this new person is we've discovered living behind this face. By the time Mandy sent Shannon down there to check on you, you were already bored with all that soul-searching. You were ready for a diversion. Of course I consider the kidnapping too much of a good thing, but it certainly added to the diversion."

"Whoa! Whoa, wait a minute. What's this about Mandy? She sent Shannon down there?"

"Yep. Of course she doesn't know I figured that out. Shannon called her the night she found you. I was home at the time. I heard enough of the conversation to realize what was going on, but if it makes Mandy feel that she's pulled one over on me, why should I deprive her of her need to gloat."

Dan started laughing. After a few minutes, Rafe joined him.

Dan got up from his chair. "I'm ready for another beer, how about you?"

Rafe checked the level in his bottle. "Sure. Why not? This is your bachelor party, isn't it?"

Dan started laughing again and headed for the kitchen. Once he returned and settled back into his chair, he said, "That makes a hell of a lot of sense. I figured that Shannon went down there looking for me, hoping for a job."

"I don't think she's that desperate. In fact, she could probably name her own salary at half a dozen places in town with her background and experience."

"I found out she used to have a crush on me when we were in school."

"No kidding? She told you that?"

"Of course not! She doesn't know I know. Buddy mentioned it. After he'd busted my chops for sleeping with his baby sister."

Rafe laughed. "What a fun-filled holiday you must have had. Glad I stayed here and worked. Vacations can be dangerous, at least the way you go about them."

"So why do you see me feeling sorry for myself tonight?"

"Well, I don't know Shannon well. Hell, I don't know her at all, but she strikes me as the kind of person who is just as you described—a modern, independent woman. I can't see her agreeing to marry anyone in order not to hurt her grandmother's feelings. And *if* she decided to back out of the wedding, I certainly don't see her doing so without calling you first."

"That would be the polite thing to do."

"Absolutely." Rafe started chuckling.

"What's so funny?"

"You sounded like some etiquette book." He mimicked, "That would be the polite thing to do."

"Well, it would."

"Mandy was right."

"About what?"

"You don't need to be alone tonight. You're dealing with pre-wedding jitters. Do you remember how merciless you were the night before *my* wedding?"

"Me? Merciless? Surely you jest. I just threw you a nice party."

"Uh-huh. And told me every one of the mean and ornery things that Mandy had ever done to you since she was born."

Dan smiled. "Ah, yes. How could I forget?"

"You kept pointing out how it wasn't too late to back out."

"I did, didn't I?"

"But you were wrong. It had been too late for months. Same thing with you. You're scared, pal. And you're not even sure what it is that scares you the most—that Shannon will back out of this wedding...or that she won't and you'll actually have to go through with it."

"Damn, that's a pathetic view of my situation if I ever heard one."

"And very normal, although you being such a super-achiever and all, I never expected to see Dan Crenshaw succumb to uncertainty. Who would have believed it? Damn. You're human, just like the rest of us. Join the crowd."

"Go to hell."

"Fine way to talk to your friend who's saving you from sitting alone in the dark, contemplating your many sins of omission and commission."

"I'm really happy that you're enjoying yourself so much."

"Say the word and I'll go home. Mandy's probably already in bed by now, but I'm sure she won't mind if I crawl in beside her and wake her up."

"Please. You're talking about my sister. I don't want to think about her getting intimate with anyone."

By this time Rafe was laughing so hard Dan was hoping he'd make himself sick. He deserved it, forcing him to look at what a complete fool he was making of himself.

He'd feel completely humiliated if it were anyone besides Rafe pointing out the obvious.

"All right. You've made your points. Now go home and go to bed with your wife, but spare me the details.

Please. And I'll go to bed. As far as I know, I'm getting married tomorrow afternoon at two p.m. with the Reverend Andy Smith officiating. I will be there at the altar waiting, unless Shannon contacts me before then.''

''And I'll be right there beside you, holding her ring for you. Just as Mandy will be right there with *her*.''

''You really think she's going to marry me tomorrow, don't you?...All right, stop laughing.''

''I wish I had taped this conversation tonight. I'd play it back for you every anniversary just to watch you squirm.''

''Go home.''

''I'll be over tomorrow about eleven.''

''Goodnight, Rafe.'' Dan didn't get up. Instead, he watched his friend leave the room still laughing and remembered all the years when he never saw Rafe smile, much less laugh.

If marriage could perform such miracles on a hardened case like Rafe, maybe it could work its magic on him, as well.

It was late and he was exhausted. He went down the hall and into the bedroom—his last night here for a few days. Tomorrow night he and Shannon would be at the condo on the island. He would focus on that and try not to think of all he had to face tomorrow before the moment when he could finally take her in his arms.

After a leisurely shower, he dried off and went to bed. It was already past midnight. It was now officially his wedding day. He reached over to turn out the light and the phone rang.

The sudden noise in the quiet startled him. It was probably Rafe with one more jab at him before going off to dreamland. He picked up the phone and said, ''All right, Rafe, what else have you thought of?''

"Uh, Dan, it isn't Rafe. This is Shannon."

Dan froze. "Shannon? What's the matter?"

"I know it's late, and I'm sorry. There's something I need to tell you."

# Sixteen

**D**an woke up early. He glanced at the clock to confirm. If he were at the island he could go walk on the beach and wait for the sunrise.

He wasn't at the beach, but he knew he wasn't going to sleep anymore.

He went into the kitchen and made a pot of coffee and willed himself not to think. About anything. Just put one foot in front of the other, he reminded himself. Get through one minute at a time. Follow his routine.

Once the coffee was made he poured himself a cup and wandered outside.

Tom already had the three hands out in the barn, saddling horses. When Tom saw him, he came toward the house. Dan stepped off the porch and walked to meet him.

"Mornin'," Tom drawled.

"Yep, looks like it."

Tom studied the sky. "Looks like it's going to be a clear day."

"Uh-huh."

"So how are you holding up?"

"I'm okay."

"You look a little green around the gills."

"Thank you for noticing."

Tom laughed.

"So what's going on?" Dan asked, nodding toward the barn.

"Aw, we're going to move some of the stock to more grass. I figured we all needed something to keep us busy."

Dan thought about going with them, but knew they'd think he was crazy.

"I got a call this morning," Tom was saying, "from a freight company. Said they had something to deliver and wanted directions. I told them how to find us, then sent one of the men down to unlock the gate. We might as well leave it unlocked, don't you think?"

"Probably. What were they delivering?"

"Didn't say."

"Well, guess I'll go make some breakfast."

Tom touched his hat in a subtle salute. "Hope you keep it down."

"Now I really needed to hear that."

Tom grinned. "Little touchy this morning, are we?"

"If I didn't know better, I'd think you and Rafe were conspiring against me."

"Not only touchy, but paranoid. Hope it's not catching," Tom said over his shoulder. He strode away, looking as though he hadn't a care in the world.

Well, neither did Dan.

Some time later—after he'd eaten a bowl of cereal, had a piece of toast, and was thinking about making another pot of coffee—he heard a large truck pull up outside. He went to the door and looked out. A large delivery van sat near the back gate.

Dan went out on the porch, then down the steps.

The driver came around the truck. "You Dan Crenshaw?"

"Yeah."

The driver went to the back of the truck and returned in a few minutes with a large, and from the way he carried it, heavy carton. "Where do you want this?" he asked.

"Just set it on the porch."

After depositing his burden, the driver came back to Dan and handed him a receipt book. "Please sign here."

He scribbled his name and watched the driver get into the truck, turn around, and leave.

Only then did he go look at the box. It was sealed, which wasn't surprising. Dan took out his pocketknife and slit open the top, then folded back the lid. He stared down into the box in disbelief. He slowly pulled up one of the bottles, unable to believe what he saw. This was a case of Dom Perignon champagne. He saw what looked to be a packing slip inside, but when he pulled it out he found it was a note.

Glad to hear you took my advice. Thought I'd contribute to the celebration.

Gianni Guardino

How the hell had he found out? Damn, the man was as bad as Shannon's grandmother—he must have his spies everywhere, too.

He almost felt sorry for Rick Taylor. Almost.

Dan returned to the house, went into his office and did some work. He found relief in the familiar details that only demanded mental concentration, not emotional involvement.

He was surprised when he heard the back door slam and a familiar voice call out. He glanced at his watch—it was already eleven o'clock.

"I'm in here," he said, moving toward the kitchen.

Rafe took one look at him and shook his head.

"What!"

"You haven't shaved."

"So?"

"You going to get married looking like that?"

"No, as a matter of fact I'm not." He rubbed his jaw. "I figure the later in the day I shave, the longer the shave will last."

Rafe laughed. "Now you're thinking. When's Shannon supposed to get here?"

"Not until two. She'll come wearing her gown and she doesn't want me to see it until the ceremony."

"What about her family? Are they all going to be here?"

"As far as I know."

"Even her grandmother?"

"Especially her grandmother."

"You're not worried Shannon will back out at the last minute."

Dan recalled the conversation he and Shannon had shared the night before and smiled. "She'll be here."

By two o'clock the wedding guests had all arrived. The caterers had been busy since midmorning setting up the folding chairs on the side lawn, near the pavilion. They'd brought in a trellis as a backdrop for the altar. The pastor had arrived. Both sides of the family were there, except for Alan, who was bringing Shannon.

All they needed was the bride.

Dan waited at the altar with the pastor and his best man. He knew that Mandy was in the house, waiting for Shannon's arrival. He heard the car pull up but the house blocked his view.

It didn't matter. He knew. He looked at Rafe and smiled.

"You finally got some color in your face," Rafe said with a grin. "I thought you were going to pass out on me any minute."

"It's the bride who faints. Not the groom."

"Could have fooled me."

The church organist had brought a portable organ and at some signal that Dan missed, started playing. The rustling and whispers from the invited guests faded away and everyone craned to get a glimpse of the bride.

First came Mandy. Dan hadn't seen what she was wearing, either. She glowed, looking as bridelike as she had at her own wedding. He noticed that she was looking at Rafe in the same sappy way, as well.

Then, from around the corner of the house came Alan Doyle, escorting his sister to her wedding.

Dan reminded himself that it would not be the manly thing to do to pass out at his first glimpse of his bride in her wedding dress.

He'd had no idea how fairylike she would look. Alan, like his brother, was a large man, making Shannon look even smaller in comparison. She had chosen to wear a simply styled dress without ruffles or flounces. It was made of white satin, with a scoop neck and long sleeves, a fitted waist and a straight skirt that came to the toes of her white satin shoes.

She was too beautiful to be real. Emotion welled up in him.

A man didn't cry at his own wedding, either.

She wore a small cap on her head, with a veil that covered half her face. He could see her mouth. Her smile was for him, alone. He waited for her to join him at the altar.

Once there they joined hands and suddenly, without warning, Dan relaxed. She had come to him of her own free will, choosing him, despite what her grandmother had said to her.

She loved him. If such an emotion could be measured—which it couldn't—he knew it would be difficult to decide the depth of feeling they each had for the other.

And so, in front of God, their friends and their families, they spoke their vows with a sense of wholeness and completion that Dan had never before experienced.

For a long period of time he had lost his belief in the goodness of people. Today he had regained it.

Several hours later Rafe wandered over to Dan and Shannon, who were watching their guests two-step to the music from the country band Dan had hired.

"By the way, Dan," he began.

Dan rolled his eyes. "What now?"

"You are the most suspicious person I've ever known. I was just going to mention that we got the whole thing on video."

"Who's we? You were standing there next to me the whole time."

"Yeah, I know. Mandy thought it would be nice to hire a professional to video the ceremony, but she didn't want to tell you in case it might make you more nervous. I told her there was no such thing as making you *more* nervous. You reached saturation point last night."

Shannon looked at him in surprise. "You were nervous?'' she asked, sounding incredulous. ''It certainly didn't show.''

He looked at her. ''Were you?''

She leaned over and stroked his jaw. ''Are you kidding? This was the culmination of every one of my adolescent dreams. I could barely restrain myself from turning cartwheels down the aisle.''

''You sounded a little nervous last night.''

''You talked to her last night?'' Rafe asked in surprise.

''Yes, Rafe,'' Dan replied with a long-suffering sigh. ''She called after you left. Pardon me for not keeping you informed of everything that's transpired in my life. Does this mean you're planning to video my honeymoon as well, so you don't miss out on anything?''

''Great idea. I'll go tell Mandy to—''

''Forget it.'' He looked at Shannon. ''And don't laugh at him. It only encourages him.''

''I need to go change if we're going to leave here before dark.''

''I'll help,'' he immediately volunteered, ignoring Rafe. He escorted her to the house, although it took a while to stop and visit with various guests. By the time they got to the bedroom where she'd left her things, he was impatient. ''What can I do?''

She turned her back. ''Unfasten me.''

When she stepped out of her dress, she wore a half-slip, a sheer bra and white hose. She walked over to the bed where she'd laid out a pants suit. ''I figured I'd be more comfortable flying in slacks than a dress.'' She wiggled into the pants, raising his blood pressure, before asking, ''Do you intend to change?''

''No. My bag is packed. I'm ready.'' Oh, boy, was he ready.

She grinned. ''Let's go.''

Tom was waiting outside with the Jeep to drive them to the airstrip. When they stepped out on the porch most of the guests were waiting to wave them off.

Shannon turned to him. "Thank you for a beautiful wedding."

"You made it beautiful, sunshine. All I did was show up."

"There was a great deal of planning that took place." She held up her bouquet of white roses and baby's breath. "The flowers, for instance. You can imagine my surprise when they arrived at my door this morning."

"About like the way I felt when Mr. Guardino's gift arrived."

They stood at the top of the stairs while the single women waited for her to throw her bouquet. She tossed it up in the air and said, "That's the last of my duties. Let's get out of here."

They were in the air when the sun began to set. The wisps of clouds turned red, purple, mauve and indigo blue. It was a beautiful and colorful end to a very emotional day.

This time when Shannon walked into his condo, she would be his wife. Nobody had better come pounding on the door for the next few days.

If they did, he intended to ignore them.

# Seventeen

$A$ full moon appeared like a giant orange ball in the east as the plane began its descent into the small airport near Port Isabel. Dan heard Shannon's gasp when she saw it. He'd been sitting in front with the pilot, but keeping an eye on her.

He should have known she would handle the flight with no problems.

As soon as they landed, he called a cab to take them across the causeway to the island.

They were now back where it had all begun.

Once they left the cab and entered the lobby, Dan waved to the night security man before escorting Shannon into the elevator. He waited until they were inside the apartment before he said, "I have a confession to make. I figure now that we're married it won't be as tough to tell you as it would have been earlier."

Shannon had gone to the refrigerator to see if there was

anything salvageable to eat while he stood in the living room, looking around. The cleaning service had done a good job with the place.

She came back in. "Confess all you want, but you aren't getting out of this marriage that easy, buster. Did you have someone place fresh food in the fridge?"

"Yep. Figured we might not want to spend a lot of time shopping."

She walked over to him and hugged him around the waist. "Okay. Confession time. What have you been keeping from me?"

He kissed her, then stepped away, leading her down the hallway to the bedroom.

"It has to do with your call last night."

She looked surprised. "What about it? Other than it was so late to be calling."

"I thought you were calling to cancel the wedding."

She dropped to the edge of the bed and stared up at him in surprise.

"Even when you explained about your grandmother's visit and her concerns, I kept waiting for you to tell me you had changed your mind."

"Oh, Dan. I had no idea. You always act so confident about everything. But I was determined to tell you how I felt before our wedding." She grinned. "Come to think of it, you did sound a little surprised when I told you how very much I love you and how glad I was you wanted to marry me."

"Actually, I was in shock. It was as though you had been reading my mind and decided to reassure me. I wondered if I was marrying a witch or a telepath."

She pulled off her jacket, then began to unbutton her blouse. "I'm hoping you'll see me as a tempting, seductive woman." She stood and unfastened her slacks. "You had me convinced that you were going to pounce on me the moment we arrived here.''

He loosened his tie and removed his jacket. ''I'm not surprised, the way I've been behaving. To be honest, I've been really worried that I would lose you if I didn't rush you to the altar.'' He watched her go to her luggage. ''What are you doing?''

''I bought this very sexy nightgown that I intend to wear.''

''Keep that thought in mind, but for now...'' He caught her up in his arms and landed on the bed with her. ''You aren't going to need anything to make you sexier to me.''

He tried to tease her with a light kiss, but she wasn't having any part of it. She returned his kiss with so much love and passion that he couldn't resist giving in to the moment.

It was his wedding night and he had waited long enough.

With economical movements he stripped out of his clothes, then removed her filmy underwear and hose. He felt like a starving beggar at a banquet, not sure where to start first.

He explored her from the tips of her toes to her ear-lobes, kissing and caressing her, learning her, watching for subtle responses that would tell him she liked what he was doing.

Before long, Dan knew he was rushing her, but he could no longer wait. ''I brought protection in case you would feel more comfortable.''

She lay in his arms, rosy and warm. ''It isn't necessary. I can't think of anything I would rather have happen than to have your baby.''

''But not right away. I want to have you to myself for a few months,'' he whispered.

She kissed him. "Whatever you say, dear."

She encouraged him every step of the way to love her. When he could no longer hold back, she welcomed him into her arms, holding him close, following his lead.

Once inside her, he lost control. She was so perfect and he'd wanted her for so long. She seemed to feel the same way. By the time he reached his climax she was right there with him.

He collapsed on the bed beside her, laboring to catch his breath. He still held her close to him. "I hope I didn't hurt you," he said.

She gave him a sleepy smile. "It doesn't matter now. I'm glad I waited to experience being a part of you."

He adjusted her head so that she was lying on his shoulder, her arm and leg across him. He wanted her again, but decided not to rush her. After all, they had all the time in the world to explore her sensuous nature.

Dan fell asleep with Shannon contentedly curled in his arms.

When she nudged him sometime later, he smiled and pulled her closer. Without opening his eyes, he sought her mouth once again.

"Uh—Dan?" she whispered urgently. "We've got company."

Her tone caught his attention more than her words. He blinked opened his eyes and discovered that his wife had a definite knack for understatement.

The bedroom lights blazed, revealing four men dressed in black commando suits and ski masks, surrounding the bed. Each man carried an automatic weapon that looked very lethal.

"What the hell?" he said, jackknifing into a sitting position. Shannon grabbed the sheet and held it to her chest.

One of the men, the one at the end of the bed, spoke.

"Just cooperate and no one will be hurt. Get dressed. Both of you." He tossed them clothing and Dan realized it was what they had taken off the night before.

"Who are you and what do you want?"

Shannon grabbed her clothes and threw the sheet over her head. He could tell she was hastily putting clothing on. She, too, must be remembering what it was like to face captors with little to no clothes.

He couldn't believe their predicament. The world had gone mad. "How did you get in here?" he demanded. "What did you do with the security?"

"You're wasting time," the spokesman said. "If you want to leave like that, it's fine with me."

Dan glanced at Shannon and saw that she was already buttoning her blouse. She'd pulled on her tailored pants and now edged off the bed. One of the men stepped back, giving her some room.

There was no way to identify them, but they were definitely threatening. He was sorry that he hadn't insisted Rafe teach him some countermoves for a time like this, but who could have guessed that this would be happening to him.

Again.

Dan jerked on his underwear and slacks and stood. He put on his wrinkled shirt, wondering if this was the end of the line for him. Yesterday he had thought that his life was just beginning—a new life with a wonderful woman. Now he realized the future might be measured in hours, rather than years.

"Let's go," the leader said.

Dan reached Shannon's side. One of the other men stepped behind them, a silent urging to move. He noticed the other men grabbed their luggage.

Oh, great. Wherever they were going, they'd have their

wardrobe with them. When anyone came looking for them, there wouldn't be much evidence that they had actually arrived.

He glanced back at the bed. There was the evidence that they—or someone—had slept there. He hoped that would be enough of a clue for Rafe to follow.

His only solace as they were herded into the elevator was to know that Rafe would never rest until he found out the truth about what had happened to them.

"Are you from Guardino?" he asked.

No one answered.

The doors opened onto the lobby. As a group they stepped out of the elevator. Dan looked around. The security guard was nowhere to be seen.

Once outside, they were hustled to the parking lot. It was dark and he didn't see the black helicopter right away but he'd heard the lazy sound of the blades slowly rotating.

The four men lifted Dan and Shannon into the belly of the helicopter, then one of them signaled the pilot and they took off.

Shannon trembled and hid her head against him. Dan felt a murderous rage that this should be happening to them. Did this have something to do with the company? Had James figured out a way to make him pay for eluding his trap?

Once again, Dan felt helpless to circumvent what was taking place. He held Shannon close and waited to see what was going to become of them.

The steady drone of the rotors and the lack of conversation lulled Dan into a light doze. He continued to hold Shannon. She'd wrapped her arms around his waist and rested her head on his chest with her eyes closed.

He stirred when the noise changed and he realized that they were descending. Since they were seated between two thugs he couldn't look out to see where they were.

He felt the soft thud as they landed. One of the men shoved the door aside and leaped down.

"Last stop," another one said. He motioned for them to get out.

Dan was the first. He reached up and helped Shannon before he looked around. What he saw surprised and confused him.

He was still staring when he saw their luggage was handed out.

The man on the ground gave him a quick salute and hopped back inside the helicopter, which immediately took off, leaving them alone.

Shannon spoke for the first time in hours. "Where are we?"

A good question. He turned in a circle, looking for a clue.

The sun was now up, shining brightly on a white beach that curved around a turquoise lagoon. Palm trees dotted the area. Lush vegetation covered what looked to be a small island.

Shannon laughed. "We've obviously been dropped on Fantasy Island."

"I'm still doing a mental check to be sure we're both still in one piece."

"They weren't rough with us."

"No, but they were damned efficient."

She looked up and down the beach. "Shall we explore?"

Dan shrugged. "It would probably help. I wonder if there are any dangerous animals on the island?"

"Well, I can certainly see that we could get some attention with a story entitled, 'How I Spent My Honeymoon.'"

"I was trying to remember if we drank anything last night that would be considered a hallucinogenic."

"Or we could be trapped in a video game," Shannon offered.

Dan started walking. The sand was soft and very fine. He had on his dress shoes from the wedding and they were soon filled with the silt, which made walking more difficult.

At least Shannon had changed into heeless slippers. She had no trouble keeping up with him.

They discovered a wide path that led into the interior of the island and looked at each other. It had been made with crushed shells and was well tended.

"Maybe somebody lives here," Shannon said.

"I'm not sure if that's good news or bad. We're trespassers."

"Certainly not by choice."

They followed the path as it wound gradually upward. When they reached the end of it, they were speechless.

In the middle of a clearing stood a house built low to the ground. There was a thatched roof and the walls were mostly glass. They walked up to the porch that covered one side.

"Look, Dan," Shannon said, pointing to the front door. There was a large sign that said, "Welcome, Dan and Shannon."

Dan walked over to the door and tapped. There was no answer. He tried the door and it opened easily. He motioned to Shannon and they went inside.

"Oh, wow," she said reverently.

At *least* wow, Dan thought. The place looked like something found at a posh tropical resort. The room was large with a kitchen bar at one end, a table and chairs for dining, and comfortable sofas and chairs arranged near large French doors that opened onto the lush landscape.

Fresh fruit was on the table. Dan walked over to the kitchen counter. There was an envelope lying there with his name on it.

He recognized the handwriting. "I'm going to kill him," Dan muttered, reaching for the unoffending envelope.

"Who?"

Dan opened the envelope and took out a sheet of paper. He began to read.

"I was afraid that the honeymoon you planned might be too tame for you after all your adventures recently, so I decided to do you a favor and liven it up.

You have fresh supplies here for seven days, when your ride home will be back to pick you up. I figured you might enjoy the privacy.

Enjoy.

Rafe"

"I'm going to kill him," he repeated for good measure.

"Rafe did this?" she asked.

"It looks that way."

"But how did he—I mean, where would he get men and a helicopter and—I don't understand."

"Good ol' Rafe hasn't always been head of security for me. I believe we've just been given a glimpse into his closely-guarded and secret past."

"He sure went to a lot of trouble." She began to look through the cabinets, the refrigerator and its freezer. "Just look at all this food. We'll probably gain ten pounds apiece just trying to eat it all.''

They explored the place. There were two large bedrooms, one on each end of the living area. Each had a mammoth bathroom attached, with both a shower and an oversized tub.

''There's not much privacy,'' Shannon said, looking outside. It's almost like living in a tropical forest with a roof over our head.''

''I have a hunch it was planned that way. We've got the whole island to ourselves.''

''Does that mean we can swim in the nude?''

Dan laughed and spun her around in his arms. ''That means we can do anything we want, starting right now.'' He walked over to the bed and lowered her to its surface. ''I don't intend to waste a single minute.''

# Epilogue

**T**he phone rang on Dan's desk and he absently answered it.

"We've got a problem," Rafe said tersely.

"Security?"

"No. Your vice president of production has decided to go into labor."

"What! Where is she?"

"We're out here in the plant. You might want to get a move on. Danny Junior has decided to make an early appearance."

"I'll be right there!"

Dan slammed down the phone and raced through the hall to the back where most of the employees worked. He charged into the large room only to come to an abrupt halt.

Shannon sat on a folding chair, her arms protectively around her middle and her eyes closed, while Rafe knelt beside her, talking to her in a low, soothing voice. He looked up when Dan arrived.

"She's a little tense at the moment," he said quietly.

She opened her eyes. They were wide with panic. "I can't have him now, Dan. I just can't."

Dan smiled and knelt on her other side. "It seems to me that our son has chosen his own birthday, honey. Let's get you into the car, okay?"

"You don't understand," she replied in her most stubborn voice, the one he knew better than to try to reason with, "if I have him three weeks early Grandmother will be convinced that we had to get married!"

Rafe coughed and covered his mouth to hide his grin.

"Babies come early all the time," Dan said in his most reasonable tone. "She'll understand."

She looked a little more hopeful. "Maybe this is just something I ate for lunch."

Rafe met Dan's eyes and gave a quick headshake before speaking. "I don't want to argue with you," he said as consolingly as possible given the circumstances, "but I don't think so. Remember, Mandy and I have gone through this twice now. This looks like the real thing to me."

"And that's another thing! We've already had a baby born today. We can't have two!"

Dan took her hand and stroked it. "Mandy won't mind if you steal a little of her thunder, sweetheart. Maybe they'll put you two in the same room once this is all over." He looked at Rafe and winked.

"They'll get them confused," she said worriedly. "Two boys born in the same day to the same family."

Rafe cleared his throat. "Well, Kevin has *my* last name, so I don't think he'll be confused with Danny Crenshaw, Jr."

She winced and rubbed the mound that was her belly. "Oh, my. Maybe it wasn't lunch after all."

Dan stood and before she could protest, picked her up in his arms and started back the way he came. His car was parked in its usual place, right outside the back door.

She let out a squeak. "I can walk!"

"I don't have time to argue with you, sunshine. I'm getting you to the hospital."

"But I'm not ready," she wailed. "I was given three more weeks before I had to do this. We haven't even finished our Lamaze classes."

"Tell Danny, honey, not me. He's the one in a hurry."

"But what if there's something wrong?"

"There isn't anything wrong. He's just impatient like his papa, that's all." Only then did Dan realize that Rafe had followed them. He moved ahead of them and opened the door for Dan.

"I'm glad I decided to stop by on my way home from the hospital," Rafe said with a smile. "Maybe I'd better follow you and make sure everything's okay before I go pick up Mama so she can see Mandy and our newest one."

Dan didn't care what Rafe did at the moment. Rafe had been up most of the night but seemed to have enough energy for all of them. He was remarkably cheerful about all of this.

Dan, on the other hand, completely understood Shannon's reaction. It *was* too soon. What if there was something wrong with the baby? Wouldn't he be too small? After the shock of finding out she was pregnant after their lusty honeymoon—despite their careful precautions—Dan had come to accept that they had started their family.

It had helped when they found out that Mandy was pregnant again. Watching Rafe and Mandy with Angie and listening to all their plans for the new arrival had helped Dan to adjust to the idea of not only a wife but also the idea of a child in a few short months.

He placed her carefully in the car, then dashed around to the other side. Rafe gave him a wave. "I'll be right behind you."

Dan nodded before he jumped into the car.

"I can't go to the hospital yet," she announced.

He smothered his sigh. "Why not?" he asked, starting the car, checking her seat belt and his.

"I don't have my suitcase. I only packed it this past weekend because I didn't have anything else to do."

That was another thing. Her pregnancy had given her superhuman energy. The woman had turned into a perpetual dynamo. She'd had the third bedroom—the room he'd used growing up—turned into a nursery, supervising each and every step. All of this was in addition to working with him during the day.

She'd been a great asset to the company with her innovative ideas and enthusiasm. He'd recently discovered that she'd saved the company thousands of dollars with a new accounting program.

He'd enjoyed sitting back and watching her these past few months as she zipped around the office and their home like an enthusiastic hummingbird. She hadn't allowed her pregnancy to slow her down in the slightest.

"I'll bring your suitcase to the hospital, honey. Don't worry. You won't need it right away."

Dan forced himself to concentrate on the traffic. Thank God it was early afternoon. He couldn't have dealt with rush hour at the moment. He glanced in his rearview mirror. Rafe was close behind them.

"Are you timing them?" he asked.

"Uh—no, not really. But I haven't had another one since we got in the car."

"Which was five minutes ago. At least I don't have to worry about trying to deliver him in the car."

"That is not amusing."

"I didn't intend it to be. Remember, I've just been learning how to be a husband these past few months. Fatherhood terrifies me."

"Oops, I spoke too soon," she said, beginning to pant.

He placed his hand on her abdomen and felt the slight drawing sensation beneath the skin. He patted her lightly. "It's going to be okay, slugger. We're here for you," he said to his son.

By the time they pulled up in front of the hospital, Shannon's forehead was beaded with perspiration. Rafe was at her side of the car in moments. He opened it and looked at them both. "Everything all right?"

"She's had two contractions on the way here."

"Right," Rafe nodded. "Let's get her inside."

Everything seemed to blur and run together after that. When they whisked Shannon away, one of the nurses told him to go scrub then meet them in the labor room where he should dress in a sterile uniform.

Dan was surprised to see his hands shaking when he covered his shoes with the silly-looking slippers.

*Oh, please, don't let me lose her. She's so tiny. The doctor's been concerned about her size and the size of the baby. Please, please let her be all right.*

As soon as he stepped into the labor room, he spotted her doctor. Thank God he'd come right over.

Dr. Trent smiled when he saw Dan. "Come join the party, Papa. The more the merrier."

"How is she?"

"She's doing great. So is your son. I'm actually relieved that he's decided to show up a little early. He's already big enough. She didn't need to have a large baby."

Dan sat down in the chair next to Shannon and took her hand. "We're going to do just fine, sunshine. We're a team. Don't ever forget that."

Daniel Edwin Crenshaw, Jr. arrived at eleven-thirty that night. His cousin Kevin, born at one o'clock that morning, was a whopping twenty-one-and-a-half hours older—and two pounds heavier.

Danny weighed in at a respectable six pounds, three ounces, despite being early. More important to Dan, there were no crises during the labor and birth.

Somehow Rafe had managed to get the women put in the same room. By the time Shannon was transferred into her bed, it was almost one o'clock.

Mandy was awake. "Congratulations," she whispered to Shannon once the orderlies left. Rafe and Dan were the only other occupants of the room.

Shannon smiled wearily. "Same to you, lady," she replied.

"You know, of course," Mandy went on, "that these two are going to be constantly comparing their sons, especially since they'll have the same birthday."

Dan said, "We don't need to compare them. They're both healthy babies. That's all that counts."

Shannon squeezed Dan's hand. "Did you get in touch with my family?"

"I spoke to your mother this afternoon, then called her back once Danny was born."

"What did Grandmother say?"

"That she'd be in to see both of you tomorrow and for you to get a good night's sleep."

"I mean about his coming so soon?"

"It never occurred to me to ask her opinion. I suggest you stop worrying about it, as well. He's here, he's a perfect picture of newborn good health and I love you to distraction. Now get some sleep.'' He leaned over and kissed her.

When he straightened he noticed that Rafe was kissing Mandy good-night.

When they reached the hallway, Dan said, ''I don't want to hear any nonsense from you about Kevin's size, you hear me?''

Rafe laughed. ''I've never said a word. The fact that he looks six months old already can't be disputed, though.''

Dan grinned. ''Can you believe this? Our sons born on the same day? I can already picture what life is going to be like around the ranch in a few years.''

''Yeah, another Crenshaw-McClain pairing. Hope they don't raise as much hell as we used to. If they do, we'll be gray before we know it.''

''I wish Mom and Dad had lived to see their grandchildren,'' Dan said.

''I'm glad we have my Mom here to be a grandma to both of them.''

They walked outside and looked up at the summer night sky. ''Who would have believed three years ago that we'd both be staid family men?'' Dan said quietly.

''I still pinch myself to make sure I'm not hallucinating all of this in some fevered dream,'' Rafe admitted.

Dan gave him a little wave before getting in the car to go home.

''Shannon?'' Mandy whispered. ''You still awake?''

''I'm drifting in and out. They gave me a shot to take the edge off. I'm feeling a little dopey.''

''I'm so glad everything turned out all right.''

''Me, too. When I started labor today, I really panicked.''

"I was thinking about you and Dan...your first trip to the island...your expressed intention of giving him hell."

Shannon chuckled. "Oh, yeah. I did, didn't I?"

"And instead, you gave him a slice of heaven. That's a fair enough trade-off for him to give up his isolation from the world, wouldn't you say?"

"He's really nervous about all the new roles he's been called on to play lately."

Mandy smiled. "He'll do just fine."

"Someday, after years and years of marriage, I'll probably work up the courage to tell him about the time I had a crush on him in school."

"Why? He doesn't need to know everything, after all. We have to keep some secrets from our men. Otherwise they'd be insufferable."

"Good point," Shannon replied. "I'll just let him continue to think that he swept me off my feet. That I never stood a chance against all that Crenshaw charm." She laughed softly. "Which is certainly the truth. And now there are two of them," she added, yawning. "What more could a woman ask for in life?"

\* \* \* \* \*

*The Callaways of Texas are passionate, proud and persevering...and Annette Broadrick brings romance readers a brand-new novel featuring more of the beloved Callaway clan. Don't miss* **CALLAWAY COUNTRY** *on sale May 2000!*

If you enjoyed what you just read,
then we've got an offer you can't resist!

# Take 2 bestselling love stories FREE!

# Plus get a FREE surprise gift!

**Special Edition is celebrating Silhouette's 20th anniversary!**

**Special Edition brings you:**

• brand-new LONG, TALL TEXANS
*Matt Caldwell: Texas Tycoon* by **Diana Palmer**
(January 2000)

• a bestselling miniseries
PRESCRIPTION: MARRIAGE
(December 1999-February 2000)
Marriage may be just what the doctor ordered!

• a brand-new miniseries SO MANY BABIES
(January-April 2000)
At the Buttonwood Baby Clinic,
lots of babies—and love—abound

• the exciting conclusion of ROYALLY WED!
(February 2000)

• the new AND BABY MAKES THREE:
THE DELACOURTS OF TEXAS
by **Sherryl Woods**
(December 1999, March & July 2000)

And on sale in June 2000, don't miss
**Nora Roberts'** brand-new story
*Irish Rebel*
in **Special Edition**.

*Available at your favorite retail outlet.*

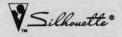